This new book was p
East Anglia Children
by Bob Able, the auth

Please give it back to a charity shop when you have read it
so that it can be sold again to make more money
for worthwhile causes!

Bobbie and the Crime-Fighting Auntie

A Bobbie Bassington Story

Bob Able

Copyright © 2023 Bob Able

All rights reserved

The characters and events portrayed in this book are fictitious. Any similarity to real persons, living or dead, is coincidental and not intended by the author.

No part of this book may be reproduced, or stored in a retrieval system, or transmitted in any form or by any means, electronic, mechanical, photocopying, recording, or otherwise, without express written permission of the publisher.

Cover Photo Credit: Dominic Sansotta & Upsplash

Bobbie & The Crime-Fighting Auntie

A Bobbie Bassington Story

By Bob Able

∞∞∞

Chapter 1

Aunt Caroline comes to stay.

Bobbie loved her Aunt Caroline.

She was the only surviving relative from her deceased father's side of the family, and although they did not see her often, it was always a cause for celebration when she left her Scottish home and visited Matravers Hall.

Now that Bobbie had a place of her own, sharing with her best friend Rosy, Aunt Caroline had shown an interest in seeing the new place and agreed to spend a few nights out of her trip with them.

Being in Wiltshire, Matravers Hall was not exactly around the corner from Bobbie's new flat on the suburban border between Hampshire and Surrey, so Bobbie had agreed to travel down in her little sports car to pick her up.

She had arranged to take three days off work for the visit and was in the process of moving into the little spare boxroom, so that her Aunt Caroline could have her more commodious bedroom, when Rosy breezed in from work.

'What Ho! What Ho! Bobbie, old friend of my youth. What's this? Moving into the boxroom?'

Bobbie explained the circumstances and Rosy offered to help as soon as she had had a shower.

'Filthy things, trains,' she said. 'I always feel grimy when I have braved the sweaty commute home!'

'Was it bad today?' Bobbie asked solicitously.

'Well, the bit on the train to here was crowded, but not too bad. But the mercifully short ride on the underground was spent pressed into the none-too-fresh armpit of a strap-hanging builder on one side and a rather tiddly businessman on his way home from a no-doubt expansive, expense-account lunch by the smell of him, on the other.'

'Yuk! How do you stand it?'

'My sweet girl, you don't think I do it for pleasure, do you? The bills do need paying.' Rosy frowned. 'Which reminds me, we really must have that little chat about your contribution to expenses and so forth.'

'Ah, yes,' said Bobbie, 'we must. But first I have news about my Aunt Caroline which I must share with you before she graces us with her presence, and I think you will like what I have to impart.'

'First the shower,' said Rosy, 'then the news from the

home front.'

And shedding her outer garments as she went, she took herself off to the bathroom.

-ooo0oo-

Roberta 'Bobbie' Bassington will be remembered as a girl of strong passions who, when roused, was quite likely to start something.

However, most of the time at least, she was a little ray of summer sunshine, full of fun, and one of those charming girls you encounter sometimes who somehow seem to make life a brighter, sweeter thing.

With her lively auburn hair, pert upturned nose, petite frame and large green eyes, she was certainly very attractive. But those mischievous eyes could also shoot flames for several feet, as some of her short-lived boyfriends had found to their cost in the past.

Now, however, settled into a more solid relationship with the charming Pedro, whom she met in Spain, her tantrums were less in evidence. But with Bobbie, you can never be quite sure when something might go off bang.

Her flat mate, Rosy Brice-Waterman, was quite different. Bobbie described her thus to her Uncle Geoff …

"Outdoorsy, all-for-it type. We were up at Girton together. She was a bit of a blood for rowing and all that sort of thing. Fearsomely bright, of course. One of those clever girls who got into University early. She was a year below me but graduated at the same time and was always heaps of fun."

This pair had had their moments, but they were now the best of friends and were having a very enjoyable time in their newly rented flat, which is where we join them now.

'So,' said Rosy, fresh and pink from the shower. 'Who, or what is Aunt Caroline?'

'Oh, you are going to love her, I'm sure. She is my late father's much younger sister and hides herself away in Scotland for most of the year. She is a freelance journalist by profession and hunts out stories of shenanigans involving people in business or Government to earn her weekly envelope. She is pretty good at it too.'

'And she is coming to stay here, you say?'

'Just for a couple of days. She will base herself at Matravers Hall for the rest of her visit, with mother. You don't mind do you?'

'Of course, not. Delighted, delighted. No problem.'

'And the other thing is that she is absolutely rolling in the stuff. She inherited at the same time as my father got Matravers Hall. He got the family home, she got the money and jewels.'

'I see,' said Rosy, interested.

'And, with no other family and never having married, she is often very generous to her favourite niece. It is she who provided the wherewithal to buy my dear little sports car.' Bobbie smiled, as she always did when she thought about her little car, which she loved with a passion.

'On the subject of money …' Rosy raised the topic again.

'Ah, well, yes. But I hadn't actually finished telling you about Auntie Caroline. She is not just here, south of the border, as it were, for a holiday. She is on a case, and from what I gather from mother, it is an intriguing one, too.'

'Something is interesting her here?' asked Rosy.

'Well, in London, actually. Mother often filches ideas for the plots of her ghastly novels from things Auntie Caroline tells her. But my Aunt lives them for real.'

'I thought your mother wrote historic romantic novels?'

'She does. Well, romantic bilge actually,' smirked Bobbie, 'but she gets ideas from Auntie sometimes which she incorporates when she needs to find a bit of a plot for some of her sloppy, supine characters to latch onto when they need a bit of back-bone.'

'Any idea what it is she is investigating?' Rosy was

fascinated now.

'Well, if I have, and I'm not saying I haven't,' Bobbie laughed, 'you should know that I'm sworn to secrecy and I should have to kill you if I told you!'

-ooo0oo-

'I think it might be an idea if you left those builders alone for a while now, Geoff,' said Janet. 'I'm sure they know what they are doing and they don't need you fussing round them.'

Since the builders had started on the extension to 2 Easton Drive to provide a double garage with a utility room at the rear, Geoff had not been able to leave them to it.

'I'm sorry, love,' he said, 'It's just that this is your house and I don't want them to mess it up.'

'It is going to be your house soon too, dear. When we are married it will be put in both our names, that's what we agreed.'

Janet was becoming impatient, and while she was very grateful to Geoff for paying for the extension, including the rather unexpected utility room that the architect came up with, along with funding a new kitchen and carpets, she wanted him to settle and feel that this was as much his home as hers.

Since they made the decision not to sell 2 Easton Drive, and now that Geoff's former marital home had when she was working on uncovering how guns from Libya came to be in the hands of the IRA, and she was lucky to escape from a burning cinema in Dublin during a fire-bombing.

After that, amid death threats aimed at the team she worked with, she left English newspapers behind and for several years worked for the BBC, based in Scotland, behind the scenes, in their political journalism team.

Today, as a freelancer, she involved herself in national and international investigative journalism. She worked closely with many organisations, including, it was rumoured, the Government's less visible agencies, the police, and the military. Now with a formidable reputation for fearlessly exposing wrong-doing, she was respected for her incisive, dependable research and she was much in demand both by the press and the television media.

She also had the most terrific sense of fun and mischief, and helped Bobbie to create mayhem at her old school, when Bobbie's turn came to attend the same establishment.

For example, when the compost heap exploded showering those nearby with rotting vegetable matter in the middle of the school sports day, it was Bobbie who organised the conflagration, but it was her Aunt Caroline who showed her how to make it happen.

They were made of the same stuff and had the same

irrepressible streak running through them, so it was no surprise that they got on so well.

As Bobbie squashed her Aunt's case into the small luggage space in her little sports car, she was excited to be in her company again and as soon as they left the gates of Matravers Hall behind them, she started to ask about the latest investigation she was involved in.

'You know, of course, that a certain elegant and charming young assistant stands ready to work alongside you, especially if this case involves you in the sophisticated and glamorous world of international society,' she offered.

'I'm not sure that you understand what the daily grind of investigative journalism involves, Bobbie,' smiled Caroline indulgently. 'It is certainly not at all glamorous. Unless, of course, spending hours working through years of newspaper archives and old police records, followed by sleepless nights sitting in cold cars waiting for something to happen is something you consider an attractive way to pass your time.'

'Well, it has got to be more creative than selling radio advertising to a dis-interested audience of unconvinced hard-boiled businessmen, at least,' said Bobbie.

'The job not going well then?' Caroline asked, 'I would have thought it was right up your street and certainly quite glamorous, compared to what I do.'

'Frankly,' said Bobbie, 'I'm finding out that flogging fluff to frozen-faced fellows with falling sales figures is not any sort of fun and I'm very bored with it. I am also not very good at it, and can't seem to convince anyone to sign up.'

-ooOOoo-

'What I can't understand is why you still do it, Caroline. It is not as if you need the money. You are, what, sixty-five this year?'

'I suppose it is a bit like a drug, Geoff,' Caroline replied, 'Something you just can't leave alone. I know I'm getting a bit old for it now, so I do hand quite a lot of the racier stuff over to my junior assistants these days, but I still can't contemplate retiring.'

Geoff had known Caroline since his marriage to Bobbie's other aunt, this time on her mother's side, and was always rather bemused by her way of earning a living. She seemed to deliberately put herself in the path of danger and led a very precarious existence where her continued success was far from guaranteed.

With a steady job in insurance in the City of London, before he took early retirement, Geoff could not understand anybody wanting to fling themselves into dangerous situations with no certainty of any reward, just to get a story to sell to the newspapers or the TV companies.

But he liked Caroline as a person and, if pressed, might admit that he had a sneaking admiration for her accomplishments. He knew she was behind exposing some big scandals that had been on the news, and that did demand respect.

Geoff's opinion of her career choices was in a minority of those present, however. As they stood now in the lounge of Bobbie and Rosy's flat, looking out at the view of the railway embankment behind the trees and the shops opposite, Caroline's life seemed exotic and different to those of the younger generation present, and also to Janet, who confessed that she had never met an investigative journalist before.

As Bobbie and Rosy handed round the drinks, Caroline looked around her.

'Well, this seems very comfortable,' she said. 'You seem to have landed on your feet here, Bobbie. And really you didn't have to move out of your bedroom to accommodate me, I can sleep on the head of a pin if I have to.'

-ooOoo-

Bobbie's boyfriend, Pedro, was in the process of moving to England to take up residence in a tiny student flat in a house on the edge of the college grounds in central London.

Bobbie had inspected it and found it small but acceptable, and considerably better than the selection of messy student accommodation she had been

BOB ABLE

Chapter 2

Over afternoon tea and toast, Bobbie asked her Aunt Caroline again what she was working on.

'Well, it might come to nothing, of course,' Caroline said, buttering a piece of toast. 'It involves some sharp practice in the world of importing cars from abroad.'

'Go on,' said Bobbie.

'Well, so far there is not much to tell, really. I've found out that some people buying new cars might not be getting what they are expecting. There are a couple of examples of new car buyers using an 'on-line' car company who are ending up with used cars.'

'How can that be? Surely there would be miles on the clock if it wasn't new.'

'That is the cleverness of this particular scam, it seems this company removes certain components and replaces them with something so that the car doesn't register the miles it has travelled. There is a link I am working on to that. You can legitimately buy nearly new-vehicles that have sometimes been used as holiday hire cars in Malta and Cyprus, for example, where they drive on the same side of the road as us, which are then sold in the UK as slightly used after a few months. But this is different and these cars are sold as brand new cars imported for buyers over here.'

'But that's horrible!' exclaimed Bobbie. 'I've never had a brand new car but I can imagine the excitement, after saving up all the money, when it finally arrives, all new and shiny.'

'Imagine how the shine would come off it if you found it had dents or scratches and smelt of cigarettes,' said Caroline. 'Some of these cars even have signs of repaired accident damage and worn tyres.'

'Surely people would notice and not accept the car?' Bobbie was astonished.

'You would have thought so, wouldn't you, but this company delivers the cars to the buyer's door and makes the buyer sign paperwork accepting it with the weasel words "as seen" and stating that it might not actually be new, buried in the small print, so the buyer has no recourse. Needless to say this company offer cars at heavily discounted prices over what you would pay for a new car at a main dealer, and that is why people go to them.'

'So how did this come to light?' asked Bobbie, intrigued.

'Someone who bought one of these cars discovered

that it was not the newest model that they thought they had ordered, and in that case it emerged that the car was actually almost eighteen months old.' Caroline reached for the teapot and replenished her cup.

'Blimey! Where had it been for all that time then?'

'Sometimes they are used as private hire taxis. Others have been rented out by holiday hire companies either in Japan, where they are built, or in other countries before they get here. The cars are actually built for the home market in Japan, rather than for export and because, as I said, they drive on the same side of the road as us there as well, it is difficult to spot any differences when certain parts are changed.'

'And you are going to expose this scandal?' Bobbie looked in awe at her clever aunt.

'Not yet, and of course you must say nothing at all about this to anyone, but I think I can find a way to identify who is behind this. This company doesn't have showrooms or even offices as far as I can establish. It's all done on the internet and they send a salesman round to the buyers' homes to do the deals. I just need a little more proof of their identities to get it packaged up in a form that will interest the authorities, and then I can sell the story.'

'I shall say nothing to anyone about this, no matter how long they torture me,' said Bobbie.

'Nobody is going to torture you, Bobbie, don't be silly,'

smiled Caroline. 'At least they won't if you keep your mouth shut about it.'

'Of course I will remain as silent as the grave, Auntie. But if there is anything I can do to help you with this, you know you only have to ask. I'd love to be involved in something as exciting as that!'

'Well, there is something, as it happens,' said Caroline now.

'Really? I'll do anything!' Bobbie squeaked.

'OK, perhaps you can make some more tea to lubricate my brain cells. That would be a great help.'

'Oh, Auntie Caroline, that is not quite I meant!'

'I know, Bobbie,' smiled her aunt, 'but it's a start.'

-ooOoo-

Geoff was making tea for the builders.

He had managed to stop himself visiting them until now as Janet had insisted, but at ten o'clock, he felt justified in breaking his self-imposed curfew.

He already knew how each of the three workmen took their tea and had a little post-it note on the fridge with their names, preferences for number of spoons of sugar, milk and so-on to hand.

Paul (two sugars, white) was the boss and tended to be the least likely to want to stop and chat. But today Geoff had a secret weapon . . . Doughnuts.

He stirred the mugs of tea and positioned them with the bag of four doughnuts on a tray and opened the back door.

The inevitable drizzle was being made more unpleasant by a gusting wind which flapped the bits of sacking and plastic sheets the builders had arranged on the brick walls they were building.

Geoff was dismayed to find only Dave (one sugar, white) working.

'Hello, Geoff, I thought you had abandoned us. I'm fair gasping for a cuppa!' he said, cheerily.

'Where are the others?' Geoff enquired.

'They will be back in a minute, they got talking to one of your neighbours and have popped over to his house to give him a quote for some work. Are those doughnuts in that bag?'

Geoff was horrified.

This was what happened if you didn't make yourself pleasant to these builders and failed to apply constant vigilance. Sneaking off to deal with enquiries from interfering neighbours, indeed.
Had he been more watchful he could have fended the neighbour off at the gate, or at least arranged matters in such a way that the builders visited them at the end of the working day, rather than leaving the job at this time.

saw the work you are having done, we felt it was time to push it along. Paul here has been giving me some advice.'

'A two-storey extension?' said Geoff, aghast.

'Yes. A granny flat for the wife's mother, a family room and a double garage with a conservatory on the back. Been rather looking forward to getting started on it, actually.'

It was Geoff's worst nightmare. The job this pesky neighbour wanted was much bigger that his own modest extension and the builders would be anxious to secure such a substantial project. He had visions of his own garage playing second fiddle to this huge construction and the delay it would inevitably cause if the builders worked on both jobs simultaneously. It would mean the upheaval to his quiet life with Janet would go on interminably. He made up his mind to speak.

'Yes, well, I'm sure my builders would be interested in a job like that, but obviously they would have to finish this work first. We have agreed a timetable and need to stick to it, you see.'

Paul, having finished his tea and doughnut felt well enough refreshed to join the conversation now.

''S no problem, Geoff, mate.' he said, wiping his mouth on his sleeve. 'If Colonel Duncan-Browne wos to give us the job, like, we would be all but finished on yer garage 'fore starting that. We cud problee speed this little job up a bit so we could get onto that, so everyone's a winnah.'

Visions of a bodged and rushed job appeared in Geoff's mind as he imagined the builders, *his* builders, hurrying to get to the more lucrative work.

'Well, I can't see …' he spluttered.

'Have no fear, old man,' Duncan-Browne, who just *would* be a retired colonel, was saying. 'If Paul and I can work up a price and programme of works together, I'm sure your garage won't be affected. I'm used to sorting out building projects. Did it in the army, building temporary staff accommodation, and all that sort of thing, you know.'

Geoff felt that his world was collapsing around him and that he was losing control of the situation. And he was sure that things were going wrong when Paul announced that he was just going along with 'The Colonel' for a walk around his garden to 'scope the job'.

'Cheerio, old chap,' said the dreadful old buffer, 'Thanks awfully for the tea and doughnut.'

-ooo0oo-

Bobbie returned Pedro's call straight away.

'Bobbie! Is you? Good. I furry excited. We got the cheap tickets chance for the cinema in the Leicester Square for the students like a me. How 'bout I taking you there on the Saturday see the block-buster movie?'

'Ooo! That would be nice, Pedro,' she said. 'What time does the film start.'

'Momento,' said Pedro and there was a rustling of paper. 'She starting the ocho, I meaning the eight o'clock. We getting the meal then going lickerty-split to the movie house?'

'Oh. In the evening? Well …'

'Is problem, Bobbie?'

'Well, that means I will have to go back home on the train late at night and on my own. I'm not sure …'

'No. Is no problema!' exclaimed Pedro. 'I think this! First the Pedro he think maybe you stay here, but you know they no say girls allowed, so we stay the hotel, but then Pedro he remember what you say. No go. The Pedro he knows this. Furry sad, but he knows. This Pedro he respect.'
There was an audible sigh before he continued.
'So then is coming the idea. You bring a the Rosy too, so you go back in the train with she. Nobody messin' with the Rosy. She scary the bums off outta there quick smart!'

'Well, that is an idea,' said Bobbie excitedly. 'I will ask Rosy what she thinks. Although it might be better not to mention to her that you think she is scary, she might be sensitive about her appearance and I would hate to upset her.'

'Hot dog!' Exclaimed Pedro. 'This the real tabasco! Yes, Siree!'

'Pedro,' said Bobbie, 'I keep meaning to ask you, where exactly did you learn to speak English?'

'My eeenglish good, no? I learning the kindergarten stuff at the school, then I listen hard to the people in the hotel where I working. Also watching the eeenglish language channels all time on the hotel TV.'

'I see,' said Bobbie,

'I learning the modern talking from the American shows they re-running. I like the Cheers, and the Starsky and the Hutch. Yays, and the Sesame Street and the old Westerns. But best is the Dukes of Hazzard, they my favourites, y'all watching them back a home too?'

'That explains a lot,' chuckled Bobbie. 'You are so funny, Pedro!'

'I not joking,' said Pedro, alarmed. 'I got chance get the cheap tickets for real, babe. I no kidding you!'

'I know, sweetie. Let me talk to Rosy and I'll call you back.'

'Yays. But Bobbie, I no got the lot of dosh, so maybe the fish and the chips first? No the slap-up meal in a posh diner ... OK?'

'Perfect,' said Bobbie, 'And of course we can each pay

for our own supper that way.'

'You no think the Pedro he the skinyflint, no treat his girl right?'

'No, Pedro. I think you are really quite marvellous. I will call you right back. 'Bye.'

-ooOoo-

Chapter 3

'The shower in the bathroom is rather good, isn't it.' said Caroline, 'The one in my cottage is hopeless, it just dribbles. No water pressure you see.'

Bobbie's Aunt Caroline was an early riser and had made a cooked breakfast for Bobbie and Rosy, much to their delight, to be ready when Rosy emerged from the bathroom as she prepared to go to work.

'I say, this is frightfully decent of you, Caroline,' said Rosy, settling herself at the table and licking her lips. 'A proper cooked breakfast is a rare treat indeed!'

'I do hold to the old saying that breakfast is the most important meal of the day,' said Caroline. 'And as your flat is actually just opposite Waitrose it was easy for me to gather up the ingredients last night before they closed, so that I could surprise you this morning.'

'Mushrooms, bacon, eggs, beans and even a grilled tomato. You are a wonder, Auntie Caroline,' smiled Bobbie, shaping her elbows and tucking in to her plateful. 'Thank you very much!'

'And nice thick slices of fresh granary bread with

proper butter. You can't beat that,' added Caroline.

'You can come to stay again!' chuckled Rosy.

'Well, I have to tell you that my motives are not as blameless as they might appear.' Caroline said now. 'You see I have little job for Bobbie and me today, which might mean we won't be home in time for supper and might have to grab lunch on the go, so a good lining now is called for.'

'A little job?' said Bobbie, intrigued.

'Well, you did say you wanted to help me.'

'Oh, absolutely! What are we going to do? Round up the baddies at the end of a chaotic car chase across the countryside, cornering them in an abandoned chalet in the Surrey hills?' squeaked Bobbie.

'I thought your mother was the one with the imagination to dream up romantic plots, Roberta, my girl. We shall be doing nothing of the kind.' Caroline smiled.

'Pity I can't join you, it sounds like fun, whatever it is,' said Rosy, wiping a little tomato ketchup from the corner of her mouth, 'but I must resume life as a wage slave in order to pay the mounting bills for this place. Which reminds me, Bobbie, on the subject of bills …'

'Yes, well, shelving that for the moment,' said Bobbie hastily. 'What are we going to be doing Auntie? Should I dress all in black and find my gloves?'

'Dress in black and find your gloves? Whatever are you talking about?' Caroline was laughing now.

'Black clothes to be invisible in the shadows and gloves so not to leave incriminating fingerprints … it was in one of Mother's novels …'

'I didn't think you read that sort of thing,' said Rosy, leaning back in her chair, replete after finishing her breakfast. 'That was wonderful Caroline, thank you. And now I'm afraid I must dash.'

'You are most welcome, Rosy. I've popped a couple of frozen microwave meals in the freezer in case you are on your own for supper, please help yourself,' Caroline stated, 'and there is fruit and some yoghurt in the fridge.'

'When did you buy all this stuff, Auntie? I didn't hear you going out last night.'

'When you were in the bathroom for almost an hour, Roberta. Honestly, you will wash yourself away!'

'And think of the cost of all that electricity heating up gallons of water,' added Rosy as she started down the stairs to leave 'Bye all, and thanks again for the breakfast, Caroline.'

As the door closed, Caroline inspected Bobbie carefully.

'Why are you not paying your share of the bills, Bobbie?'

'Who says I'm not? I just have a temporary pause in my fiscal flow which will finish soon, I hope, and then I can shower Rosy with my bounty.'

'How much do you owe Rosy?'

'Oh, it's just little bagatelle really. My own fault, of course. You see the car needed a service and then there was this sale on at the dress shop on the corner and ...'

'How much, Roberta?'

'It's not that I won't get paid soon, it's just that until I get some commission coming in the basic salary is a bit ...'

'Roberta!'

'I owe my share of a month's rent, two do's of weekly shopping and my half of the last quarterly electricity bill.'

'I see.'

'Yes, but if I give Rosy all my wages at the end of this month and put the car service on Uncle Geoff's account at the garage, that will leave me only owing a mere trifle ...'

'And when might you expect some commission to come through, young lady?'

'Well, that is rather the nub or root of the problem, you see, Auntie. It doesn't seem to matter how hard I try, I have to admit that I'm complete rubbish at selling radio advertising to anyone. I haven't actually made a single sale since I started there.' Bobbie blushed and, shamefaced, studied the pattern on the table cloth.

'So your basic salary is not enough to cover your bills then?'

'It nearly is, so long as there are no other expenses.'

'Like sales at the dress shop, I suppose?'

'Ah, yes. Something in that, I suppose. But you see there was this adorable little black dress with long sleeves and lace at the cuffs, and Pedro is taking us to the cinema in Leicester Square, so I ...'

'Yes. I think I get the picture.' Caroline took a deep breath. 'Of course I expect to pay you for your work with me over the next couple of days, so ...'

'Oh. no, Auntie, I couldn't! I wouldn't dream of ...'

'Yes, you would, you little minx, but you will have to earn it.'

'Oh, Auntie, I'll do anything. My elegant and shapely fingers will be at your disposal to work to the very bone. I shall not spare any effort ...'

'Right,' smiled Caroline. 'You can start by doing the washing up!'

-oo0Ooo-

'I have met this Colonel Duncan-Browne. His name is Cyril, isn't it?' Janet was tapping her foot impatiently, 'He is, or was, a Parish Councillor and a right little Napoleon. He led the complaints about people parking on the road outside the Dentist's surgery before we pretty much *had* to buy that bit of land next door for a car park. Talk about a vested interest! His wife's mother owned the land so he was pushing us into buying it!'

'What? You mean that little strip of tarmac where I pull in when I pick you up from work?' Geoff was astonished.

'Yup, that's it. Parking for four cars. It was once part of her garden. She lives in that big bungalow next door.'

'Not for much longer,' said Geoff. 'There is going to be a granny flat for her to live in over Duncan-Browne's new garage, so she is going to be our neighbour.'

'Oh, Lordy!' said Janet, 'She is a horrible piece of work. In the past she would sometimes throw bags of rubbish over the fence. They invariably split open, of course, so that we had to pick it all up and put it in our commercial waste bins. She did it late at night so she didn't think anyone would see, but when we got the CCTV installed at the surgery it recorded her doing it, and we reported her to the Police!'

'Good heavens!' said Geoff. 'Does she still do that?'

'No, not any more. That was a few years ago. Now she is older, the bin men collect her bins from her door so she doesn't have to wheel them down to the road. She was doing it then so she didn't have to fill her bins up and then move them.'

'By the sound of things, she will be selling that bungalow now,' Geoff observed.

'I don't think so. There has been a 'To Let' board on it since she broke her hip and went into hospital. Presumably she is not going back there permanently, but when this granny flat is built she will be our neighbour here, if what you say is right.'

Geoff thought that he might not have been able to avoid the granny flat being built for ever, but perhaps if he had been a little more diligent in keeping an eye on the builders, it might not have been set to be built quite yet. He resolved to watch them like a hawk from now on.

'I'm sorry, Janet. I don't think there is much we can do about it. But maybe now she is older and is under Duncan-Browne and his wife's care, she will be a bit nicer to live near. We might never even see her.'

'I do hope not.' Janet was grinding her spectacularly enhanced teeth. 'Do you know she used to have a local charity meeting at her house every month or so in the late afternoon, before the surgery shut for the day, and she used to tell the visitors to park in our car park! She has the cheek of the devil!'

'So she took the money for the land you made into a car park for the dentist's surgery, but still thought she could use it?'

'And,' Janet said, coming to the boil, 'I shouldn't say this, but we had to take her to Court because she hadn't paid her dentistry bills for over three years!'

'Gracious! Presumably you don't treat her any more?'

'No, thank goodness. She goes somewhere else now, I suppose, because we took her off our list.'

Janet stomped off into the kitchen and Geoff, deciding that it might be prudent to be elsewhere for a while, took himself off to have a chat with the builders.

-oo0Ooo-

Chapter 4

In the little sports car, as they fought their way through the London traffic, Caroline laid out her plan and explained a little more about the task before them.

'You see, all cars have a Vehicle Identification Number stamped into the body somewhere and they have an identifying mark as to where the car is first used. In Japan, the first letter of the V.I.N. is a 'J' so it is obvious where they come from. The company selling them in the UK make no bones about the fact that these cars are imports, that is why they are cheap, but that same V.I.N. plate also identifies *when* the vehicles are built.'

'So that is how the buyers find out they are not new?' Bobbie said, weaving her way around some trucks.

'Yes, although they don't usually find out until the car goes in for a service or breaks down, when a mechanic may point it out. Look Bobbie, we are not in that much of a rush. Can't you slow down a little, please.'

'Sorry. So tell me again what I have to do.'

'Well, we are going first to a house in Kensington. The owners are not using it at present but they have told me where to get the key. That is where you will pretend to live, so familiarise yourself with the layout and make coffee in the kitchen so you know where everything is. That reminds me, we must pick up some milk as there will be none there and you are bound to need to offer the salesman a drink.'

'And tell me again where you will be.'

'I'll be outside in the car, parked as close as we can to the house, so I can see them coming and get some pictures.' Caroline shifted the heavy bag on the floor between her feet, which Bobbie knew held a professional standard digital camera with a long lens.

'But...'

'Don't worry, Bobbie. I will be able to see you all the time. The house is rigged with CCTV cameras everywhere that I can watch on my mobile phone.'

'Blimey! Did you put them there?'

'Erm, no. The owner of the house did.'

'Who is this mysterious chap then, that he needs his house rigged out with spy cameras?'

'Actually, Bobbie, you have no need to know, but you are not far from the truth there. This house is rather special, as you will see.'

'I thought you said it was just an ordinary Victorian terrace in a street of similar houses?'

'It is. Wait and see.' Caroline winced as Bobbie pulled out and hurtled past a bus, dodging back in to the left lane as cars coming the other way flashed and hooted their horns. 'Please can you slow down a bit, Bobbie!'

'Right-ho,' said Bobbie, as there were no more opportunities for overtaking in evidence. 'So I've got to kid on that I am interested in buying one of these dodgy imported cars, then?'

'Yes, you will explain that you have recently graduated and got your first job …'

'Well. that bit is true …'

'And that you have saved enough to buy a small new car but can't afford the showroom prices.'

'And then I say I had found out about possibly importing a car from a friend of a friend …'

'Quite correct, Bobbie, and you will ask questions about …'

'Whether the cars they sell are right hand drive, are British registered and with speedometers that read in miles per hour …'

'Well done. And towards the end of the meeting …'

'I will ask him just to confirm that these are actually new cars. That being the point on which he may incriminate himself.'

'That's right. Now I'll say again, if you feel uncomfortable at any point, or want assistance, just press the little button on the fob I will give you which you should keep in your pocket out of sight, and I'll be there in a flash. And if you feel the need to get away, the French doors will be unlocked and you can go out into the garden and through a back gate onto another road.'

'Yes, you explained all that, Auntie Caroline. Gosh, this is exciting!'

-ooOoo-

Janet watched indulgently through the kitchen window as Geoff heaved the lawnmower out of the shed.

For as long as she could remember, the garden of 2 Easton Drive had been tended by old Mr Prentice, or "Puffing Billy" as she and her mother had affectionately called him behind his back.

Assisted these days, at least as far as mowing the lawn was concerned, by his grandson Derek, old William Prentice had been a fortnightly visitor to the house since Janet was very small.

Today however Derek had a cold, so Geoff volunteered to mow the lawns while 'Puffing Billy', so called because of the ever-present cigarette clamped between his teeth, pottered about tending the roses and hoeing in some weeds that had the temerity to put in an appearance on the edge of a flowerbed.

Geoff liked Mr Prentice and had been invited into his shed on more than one occasion.

This was a rare honour indeed, and now she came to think about it, Janet was sure that she had not actually been inside this holy place more than twice in her entire life.

Beyond the firmly locked door, and all but invisible through the small grimy window, amongst the spades and rakes and several generations of retired lawnmowers, there sat Billy's most prized possession. It was a small two-ring gas stove, on which was set an elderly and much dented kettle and a little saucepan that he used to warm up soup when the weather chilled his old bones.

The gas rings were also used to light his endless procession of roll-up cigarettes, and to one side the paraphernalia for the construction of these thin and foul-smelling things lay, set out just as he liked them, ready to prepare yet another gasper.

There was an old, rickety kitchen chair which had once been painted red, in the days when loud colours were all the fashion, on which Billy took his ease or sheltered from the rain, and on a nail hung a wax coat and a very tired tweed cap.

Billy had two caps. The one which was habitually on his head wherever he went, and only ever partially removed to scratch an itch or to assist thought, and the one on the nail, used when working in the garden itself.

The older cap had several tears in the cloth and incongruously, considering its work in the garden, several tied flies used for fishing hooked into the fabric. It was these fish hooks which had started the conversation that first enabled Billy and Geoff to form their gentle friendship.

Although, since his first wife took over control of his social calendar and there had been little time for him to indulge in any hobbies, Geoff had once been a keen fly-fisherman. Seeing the old lures in Billy's cap gave him the opportunity to ask if this worthy old chap still indulged in the piscatorial arts himself.

That led to Billy inviting him into the shed where, in a dusty corner, he kept a selection of fly-fishing rods and an ancient box of tackle, which he shyly allowed Geoff to examine.

Billy explained that although now semi-retired, he had not found time to indulge in the pastime and was hampered by the fact that there was no fly- fishing water within easy reach of his elderly bicycle, and he did not possess a car.

Geoff thought of his own quite extensive collection of fishing tackle, bundled up in a corner of the little low-roofed, brick-built shed by the back door which had originally served as a coal store when 2 Easton Drive was first constructed, before the almost universal adoption of gas-fired central heating; and as the pair spoke of past glories and "the one that got away" as old fishermen tend to do, a plan started to emerge.

Billy and Geoff had decided that, when the fly-fishing season started, they would travel together in Geoff's car and spend a day revisiting their shared former passion. But there was a problem, and Geoff wondered if he had been a little rash.

Nobody had ever smoked in Geoff's precious Jaguar, and he did not want to offend Billy, but he now had to find a way to ask if he would mind keeping his cigarettes in his pocket until they reached the riverbank, and he was struggling to think of a method by which to pose that awkward question.

Volunteering to mow the lawn in place of Derek, Billy the gardener's grandson who usually did it, and who was was recovering from a cold, was Geoff's method of building up to this tricky moment. Perhaps, he explained to Janet, if he made the old chap feel slightly obligated to him he would be more amenable to shelving the smoking during the journey.

Janet had laughed at this suggestion, which Geoff took to mean that she thought he was unlikely to succeed in his efforts to convince Billy not to smoke, particularly when she explained that, come rain or shine, she had never seen Billy without one of his foul roll-ups in his mouth.

But Geoff had to try. The Jaguar was, after all, very dear to him and he hated the thought of the fine polished-leather smell it exuded being tainted by smoke. So he nerved himself now for the conversation to come, as he manhandled the lawnmower out of the shed and prepared to mow.

-ooOoo-

It was as well that the milk they bought from a corner shop was very cold as the fridge in the house was not turned on and would take too long to cool down.

'Right,' said Bobbie, turning round with two mugs in her hand as she closed one of the kitchen cupboard doors. 'I've found the tea, coffee and sugar so I think we are ready to go.'

'Remember, Bobbie, if you are asked, this is your parents' house and they are out at work. I think it is time we familiarised ourselves with the layout and woke the house up while the kettle boils.'

'Woke the house up? What do you mean?'

'I'll show you,' said Caroline taking what looked like a TV remote control from one of the kitchen drawers. 'Watch.'

'The bay window first, I think.' Caroline pointed the controller at the closed curtains of the front window which, to Bobbie's surprise gave a twitch and then started to draw back.

'Flash!' said Bobbie. But then she became aware that behind the curtains were very substantial looking shutters which also started to move back with a creak.

Bobbie walked towards the window for a closer look.

'These shutters are thick solid metal,' she said, 'They look like wooden ones but they are not!'

Caroline chuckled and pressed another button which made the curtains over the French doors open to reveal more solid shutters which also began to fold themselves up.

'What is this joint?' asked Bobbie. 'Who needs solid steel shutters at their windows?'

'Solid steel bullet-proof shutters, actually. I had better tell you a little bit about this place.'

'Er, yes. If you wouldn't mind. It's like something out of a spy novel.'

'And you haven't seen the half of it yet.' Caroline was pressing more buttons and a small panel on what Bobbie thought at first glance was an old fashioned drinks bar, opened with a beep to reveal a series of controls and dials, a bit like a professional hi-fi system.

'This is what is called a safe house, Bobbie. It is used for short periods to provide secure accommodation for certain people who may need to have some protection.'

'Safe house? Who owns this place, Auntie Caroline?'

'The Government, my dear. Now don't be alarmed. I'm only borrowing it for today because I happen to know someone who organises its use. It is quite unofficial really. That console you see over there,' she said, pointing at the dials and knobs in the drinks bar, 'controls the microphones, video and so on which I shall be using to keep an eye on you on my phone in the car.'

Bobbie tried to swallow the lump in her throat.

'This is scary, Auntie Caroline. I had no idea you got involved in stuff like this, and you seem to know how it all works too.'

'I've used the house before, Bobbie. I stayed here once, years ago and before all this technology was installed, so I'm quite familiar with the layout and my friend in the Government office showed me how this equipment works.'

'Wait a minute. What Government office? Why would you need to stay in a safe house?'

'Time is getting on, Bobbie. I'll explain all that later. Just trust me for now, eh? Now here is the key for the French doors and I'll go out the back way and unlock the gate in case you need to use it.' Caroline checked her mobile phone which showed a picture of the room they were in, and moved to close the door to conceal the controls in the drinks bar.

'Take a wander round upstairs and use the loo if you need to. The salesman will be here soon.'

'But I...'

'Oh, and put this in the pocket of your jeans, Bobbie,' Caroline took a slim oval-shaped device from the top of the drinks bar 'This is the little button I told you about. Just press that if you need to and I'll be in here in a trice.'

'Auntie Caroline ...'

'Now, come on, Bobbie, nothing is going to go wrong. I just need to get some pictures of this guy and hopefully we can follow him when he leaves to find out where their office is, but you stay here until you hear my voice through the speakers telling you to come out.'

Then the doorbell rang.

Caroline squeezed Bobbie's hand as she gave her the little button to put in her jeans pocket, and before Bobbie could say anything else she was off through the French doors and out of the back gate.

Although Bobbie was very tempted to run after her, she took a deep breath and tried to quell her nerves, as she prepared herself to answer the front door.

As she opened it she found herself facing, not the swarthy salesman she had been expecting, but a short, round, middle-aged woman with blond hair and a little briefcase tucked under her arm.

'Hello, luvvy. Not too early am I? The traffic was actually only moderately awful so I got here quicker than I thought. Charley, Charley Jones,' and she held out her hand to shake. 'Come in, shall I?'

-ooOoo-

Walking up from the station, Rosy noticed that the flat was in darkness so she knew that Caroline and Bobbie were still out.

Rather than settle down to a microwave 'ping meal' alone, she walked on past the flat up to the parade of shops, where she called in to get take-away fish and chips, instead.

As she was coming back she noticed one of those breakdown company tow-trucks driving down the street and on the back was Bobbie's little sports car!

Rosy hurried down the road and arrived just as the tow-truck driver was opening the gates behind which Bobbie always parked, and Bobbie herself was standing on the pavement looking cross.

'Hello, Rosy,' she said dully. 'Had a nice day?'

'Well, it doesn't look as though you have. What happened?'

'Is that fish and chips you have got there? Can I nick a chip, I'm famished.'

As Rosy unwrapped a corner of the paper so that Bobbie could extract a chip the tow-truck operator was lowering the back section of the truck and saying that the sports car could now be pushed off on to the road.

'It's handy you are here to help push, Rosy,' said Bobbie. 'I ran out of petrol in simply the most inconvenient place imaginable and had to call the breakdown service to come and rescue me.'

'It's a good job you had breakdown insurance then …' Rosy had noticed the company logos on the side of the tow truck.

'Yes, and Dave here thoughtfully bought out some petrol in the hope of getting us going again, but the car didn't like the flavour of it or something and Dave said there was sediment in the tank that was blocking the pipes up, so we couldn't get it to go.'

'Hence the ride on the-tow truck, I see. Fortunate that you had paid for their services.'

'Oh, yes. Uncle Geoff sees to all that. He insists I have breakdown cover and makes the cost part of my Christmas present every year.'

'Where is Caroline?' said Rosy, noticing that there was nobody else in the passenger seats of the truck.

'That is a long story, which I shall tell you when we have got the car safely tucked away, thanked Dave for all his kindness, and we are eating the rest of those fish and chips together inside.'

-ooOoo-

Chapter 5

With the car safely in its parking space and a message left for Gary, her Uncle Geoff's tame mechanic on his answer phone, to come and sort out the sports car in the morning, Bobbie returned from the kitchen carrying the plates containing their shared fish and chip supper.

'Good job I got a large cod and they are generous with the chips there,' said Rosy. 'I would have got two portions if I had known I was sharing.'

'Sorry, Rosy, next time it will be on me.'

'Well, come on then. Tell me all about what happened and what you have done with Caroline.' Rosy was intrigued to hear what had been going on, and Bobbie, through a mouthful of chips began her tale.

'Um, yes, um. The house was amazing, but I'll come back to that in a minute,' said Bobbie gulping down her mouthful and preparing to take another. 'The awfully embarrassing thing was afterwards, when Auntie Caroline wanted me to follow a car, and we hadn't gone ten metres when the poor little sports car coughed and spluttered and the engine died. I'm afraid Auntie Caroline got rather cross when I couldn't get it to start again, and said some harsh things about my being inattentive as far as the lights on the dashboard were concerned. How was I to know what that yellow one meant? It had been on for ages and I just thought it was there to light up the little dials or something.'

'So you couldn't give chase?'

'No.'

'Well, that must have rather spoiled the adventure.'

'Well, in a way I suppose it did, but I said I would tell you about the house and what happened there before the funny little Welsh woman arrived ...'

'Funny little Welsh woman?'

'Yes. You see I was expecting to open the door to your standard oily salesman in a shiny suit, but they sent a woman instead. It was easy to see how the confusion arose. The email Auntie Caroline got, said to expect a C. Jones, but what we got was a Charley, spelt with an 'e' and a 'y' on the end and probably short for Charlotte, although we didn't go into that, rather than the male version spelt with an 'i' and an 'e', you see.'

'Fascinating, but what was this all about?'

'Oh, sorry, you don't know the background do you? I'll

explain … where should I start?'

'I always find the beginning is as good a place as any. Take it from the moment we finished our breakfast and I left the scene for an honest day's toil to put food on the table this evening.'

'Yes, well, thanks for that. Anyway starting, as you suggest, at the beginning, We drove to London …'

'With the little yellow light twinkling away on the dashboard?'

'With, as you say, that wretched yellow light gleaming dimly. We went to a fairly ordinary-looking house …'

'I thought you said it was amazing?'

'It was ordinary on the outside, but it was what was indoors that was so terrific. It was all rigged out with electronic spy stuff. Hidden cameras, microphones, and bullet- proof window blinds that slid aside at the touch of a button.'

'You're making it up!'

'I'm not, honestly. It emerged that Auntie Caroline had once lived in this house and knew about all this gear. Which reminds me, I must get to the bottom of why she came to be living there …'

'Perhaps someone else was paying the rent.'

'Or perhaps she had a boyfriend who was an international man of mystery who needed protection from the bad guys out to hunt him down …'

'Stick to the story you started, Bobbie.'

'What? Oh, yes. Sorry. Well, this little dumpy Welsh woman came to the door and said she was the salesperson we were expecting, although by that point Auntie Caroline had legged it through the back gate and left me to deal with her.'

'She wasn't there?'

'No, but that was all right because she was watching the cameras in the house on her mobile phone and could hear what was going on through the hidden microphones.'

'You *are* making this up …'

'I'm not, I promise. Anyway I made the little Welsh woman tea and we started to go through all the questions Auntie had asked me to get across. It was all going very well until I started, as planned, to say I thought it was too expensive and I couldn't afford it, and she got a bit shirty with me …'

'That doesn't sound a very good sales technique.'

'No, well she kept saying she had already told us the prices by email and that it had been explained that they didn't offer finance, and she said, "I haven't come all this way to discuss the prices, luvvy." She kept calling me luvvy, "I'm just here to agree the specification you want and sign the initial order form". Well, I wasn't having that, so I did what Auntie C had suggested and turned on the waterworks.'

'You started crying?'

'That was all part of the plan. You see I had to make out that I had been saving up ever-so hard since I graduated and couldn't afford a new car any other way, and give out that I was heartbroken but there was no way I could afford it, once you took into account all the taxes and whatnot that she had been explaining had to be paid.'

'I see. And did she soften?'

'Not a bit of it. She started packing up her papers and saying I was wasting her time. So then I asked the killer question.'

'The what?'

'I said that I supposed I would have to settle for a secondhand car now and wasn't it true that these cars were brand new, so that is why there were all these taxes to pay. And she said, "Yes", which was what we wanted, and something about she hadn't got time to deal with bits of girls who hadn't got a clue what they were talking about … and then she left.'

'Bit rude.'

'Oh, no. It didn't matter a bit. As soon as I had closed the front door after her I nearly jumped out of my skin when Auntie Caroline's voice came through the speakers as clearly as if she was standing next to me.'

'The speakers?'

'The hidden speakers, I thought I told you about them.'

'You did, but I didn't believe you.'

'Well you should be a little more trusting. Dismiss this suspicious attitude. It does not do you credit.'

'Get on with the story and perhaps you can dispel my doubts that this is all make-believe.'

'It's all true, I promise!' Bobbie pulled a face. 'Auntie Caroline said I had done well and to take the remote control out of the kitchen drawer and press the red button.'

'The red button?'

'That is what she said. So I did, and the bullet-proof blinds started shutting and so did the curtains.'

'Of course they did.'

'They did, I tell you. And then Auntie Caroline told me to grab the milk.'

'What milk?'

'The milk from the fridge, of course. … And to come out and run to the car where she was waiting.'

'So you made sure you had the milk, then?'

'Yes, and as I dashed across the road, she was putting her great, big, long-lens camera back in the car and climbing into the passenger side.'

'I see.'

'So I jumped in the driving seat and she said, "Quick, follow that grey BMW." And that was when I couldn't get the car to go.'

'But you had the milk. Perhaps the car wanted a drink of milk.'

'Oh, stop it! You don't believe a word of this, do you?'

But at that moment the front door bell rang, and waiting outside was a very disheveled-looking Auntie Caroline clutching her camera bag and half a pint of milk.

-ooo0oo-

'I got them, Bobbie! I getting the tickets. The good seats, too!'

'Well done, poppet. Rosy and I are looking forward to it. It looks like a good film too.' Bobbie was dancing round the living room on the tips of her toes as she spoke to Pedro on Facetime on her iPad.

'Woah, Bobbie. I'm wishing you stop doing the jumping about. You making the Pedro feel wheezy!'

'Sorry, sweetie, I forgot. And don't you mean queasy?'

'Yays, like I a say. Wheezy. Also the picture, he doing the jumpy and break up. Pedro he no see the lovely Bobbie so good, and you know the Pedro like a see the Bobbie.'

'Ahh, bless you, sweet boy! Is that better?' said Bobbie, plonking herself down on the sofa.

'Yays, but now I got go. Got the a most important meeting with the top honcho. The beeg boss, he coming down see the estudents introduce. He the Chiefy Sective. I sited but a furry bit the nervous too.'

'Just smile your lovely smile and bat your gorgeous eyelashes at him and you will have him eating out of your hand, I'm sure,' laughed Bobbie.

'I not want him eat the Pedro eye a lashes,' laughed Pedro. 'My Bobbie, she like a them, so keep just for she!'

'Oh, Pedro,' sighed Bobbie. 'I do … I mean I think I had better let you go now.'

'I love you too, Bobbie. Furry, furry much,' said Pedro, but Bobbie had cut the connection.

-ooo0oo-

Janet stood in what would become her new utility room, behind the garage.

There was still a lot to do. The plasterer had just finished but there was nothing on the floor and the wiring and plumbing had yet to be connected up, let alone the installation of the cupboards and decoration.

Geoff, however, was very pleased with the spacious double garage, which needing no plastering or any decorative finishes, was just waiting for the wiring to be completed to be ready to accommodate their cars. That was of course, when all the builders' equipment that virtually filled up the space, was removed.

'Hang on,' said Janet, stepping through the opening where the door from the utility room would be. 'What's all this?'

She was pointing at some new windows leaning on one of the garage walls.

'All the windows are fitted, aren't they? What are these for?'

'I have no idea,' said Geoff, mystified.

'And there are some metal beams and paving slabs over there. What are they for?'

Geoff examined the items carefully and came to a conclusion.

'I'll roast them alive!' he said, as a dangerous look came to his reddening features. 'The nerve of it!'

'Pardon?' said Janet.

'These materials are for that son of a bachelor, Duncan-Browne, down the road. The builders have stored them here in our new garage!'

'What?'

'The cheeky blighters!' exclaimed Geoff. 'I thought there was rather a lot of stuff being unloaded from that last lorry. They have had his materials delivered here!'

'But why would they do that, Geoff?'

'Because then they can store them in the dry without having to clutter up ruddy Duncan-Browne's house, of course! You wait 'till I get my hands on that Paul on Monday morning!'

'Geoff, darling, you are getting very red. I think you had better sit down before you pop!' said Janet solicitously.

-ooOoo-

Chapter 6

'That's not Charley Jones!' said Detective Sergeant Morris. 'That's Linda June Williams, or I'm a Dutchman. I thought she was in Holloway doing three years for fraud.'

'Well, best you check, Jack,' said Caroline, gathering up the photographs. 'If you are right and she is involved in this, I'm guessing she will soon be on her way back there.'

'I certainly will, Caroline. This is all most interesting. I'm not sure what we can do though until you can find out where this lot operate from. It is very difficult to track down these internet-only types.'

'I thought you were going to say that, and I was this close to finding out,' Caroline held finger and thumb close together for his inspection. 'If it had not been for a ridiculous situation with my silly young niece running out of petrol.'

'How so?' asked the policeman, so Caroline told her the story.

'And when I got back to her place, after a lengthy and expensive taxi ride, trying and failing to track them down, and then another one back to her flat, I might add I gave her *what for* I can tell you!'

DS Jack Morris chortled as he pictured Caroline, usually the dynamic, highly organised, high-flying investigative journalist, at a loss. She was frequently involved in unravelling shenanigans among the cleverer criminal classes as she bought them to book. And now here she was, stymied by something as commonplace as running out of petrol in a residential area of Kensington at the beginning of a promising surveillance operation.

'Stop it, Jack. It wasn't that funny.'

Following further pleasantries and once enquiries about mutual friends and acquaintances had been exchanged, Caroline wished her favourite policeman well, gathered up her photographs and took her leave.

There was much to do before this particular case could be concluded, but with Jack interested and keen for more information, she knew she was onto something good.

-ooOoo-

'Are you sure you won't mind being on your own for the evening, Caroline,' said Rosy. 'You must think we are very rude.'

'Not at all, Rosy dear, you go and enjoy the film. To be honest I've got quite a bit of work to do so I won't be fit company anyway. You have a lovely time and don't worry about me.'

'Can you help me with this zip, Rosy,' said Bobbie, standing in the doorway of the boxroom. 'It must be all those chips we ate, I think. This dress was not so tight in the shop, I'm sure.'

Rosy, still in her dressing gown and freshly showered, went to help her friend.

'We don't need to leave for another half an hour, Bobbie. I'm surprised you are so ahead of time,' she said.

'Only half an hour! Oh, gosh! I'll never be ready!'

'Well, you look pretty ready to me,' said Caroline, joining the girls in the hallway. 'I do admit that is a very fetching little dress, even if it is rather too short, to my old-fashioned way of thinking. Not that you will take any notice of what I have to say.'

'Too *short*?' said Bobbie. 'I was thinking of asking them to turn it up a bit!'

'Hmmm,' said Rosy. 'Costly, too.'

'And what are you wearing? One of your designer-label ensembles, no doubt?' said Bobbie, wrinkling her nose.

'Mother happens to like quality and feels I should make the best of myself when on public display, no doubt in the hopes of marrying me off. It's not my fault she likes to splash out occasionally on me. And I never know what to put on anyway.' Rosy wrinkled her nose back at Bobbie. 'As you well know, if it was up to me I would always be in dungarees and wellies and up to my armpits in horse muck.'

'To each their own,' chuckled Caroline. 'Come on then, Rosy, let's have a look in that big wardrobe of yours and see what we can find to ensure you knock 'em dead in London's trendy theatre land tonight!'

-ooo0oo-

'Wewl, we was only leaving it there over the weekend, Geoff, mate, just to get it in the dry, like.'

Under Geoff's furious stare, Paul was shrivelling up like a dry leaf.

'I don't care if it was only five minutes! You didn't even have the common courtesy to ask if you could store materials for another job in our house, Paul. That is just not on!'

'Sorry. Look, we will get it all moved tomorrow, all right?'

'No, Paul, I think you should get it moved today!'

'But I'm all on my own today, Geoff, and that stuff is

heavy.'

'Oh, yes,' said Janet, appearing at Geoff's side. 'And where are the other two then?'

'Erm … They are …'

'And if you are going to say they are working at Colonel Duncan-Browne's house, after you agreed that you would not start there until you finished here, I will want to hear why!'

'Wewl,' said Paul sheepishly, 'the idea was they was coming on here after doing a bit of prep there, if there was time.'

'I suggest,' said Janet, drawing herself up to her full height, 'that you ring them up and get them back here right now. And you can consider yourselves very lucky that we have not thrown you off the job!'

'But … But … The Colonel said if we couldn't start straight away he wouldn't give us the job, so we …'

'Decided to go back on your word to us!' said Janet coldly.

'And it better not happen again,' said Geoff turning on his heel, linking his arm through Janet's, and heading for the kitchen. 'And if you think you are getting any more tea, let alone doughnuts, you have another think coming!'

'Well done, Geoff, darling,' smiled Janet, shutting the kitchen door behind them. 'I didn't know you had it in you!'

-oo0Ooo-

'You liking the popcorn, Rosy?'

'Oh, I say, rather! The sweet kind I think, please, Pedro.'

'Bobbie?' said Pedro, although he hoped the answer was going to be in the negative.

'No, thank you, Pedro, sweetie. I've just seen the price of that stuff. It's daylight robbery!'

'No, actually, cancel that,' said Rosy. 'You are right about the extortionate prices they charge in these places, and I want to encourage this new fiscal responsibility we see developing in young Roberta here!'

'Also no rot a the teeth out now with that,' smiled Pedro, relieved.

'Just as you say. No point damaging the dental equilibrium for a few moments of sticky pleasure that, no doubt, we will be picking out of our teeth long after the film has finished.' Bobbie smiled to show that her teeth at least were in fine fettle.

'Quite,' said Rosy and looked at her wrist watch. 'Shall we be finding our seats? The film is not quite ready to start, but I do think the adverts and short clips beforehand are a hoot, don't you? You get the best bits of at least three other films in the trailers, so you don't have to shell out to see them and waste any more money on cinema prices.'

'They coming on the telly soon enough,' said Pedro. 'Watch there is no so spensive.'

'Oh, Pedro, were the tickets frightfully expensive?' asked Bobbie, suddenly embarrassed.

'I telling. Got the estudent discount from a the college so no big deal. But not the everyday. I been the cinema before many times, this not my first rodeo, I knowing how spensive is the normal.'

'Well thank you very much for sharing your discount with us,' said Rosy graciously as she opened the swing doors leading to the main event with a flourish. 'Shall we?'

Chapter 7

Caroline was up some time before the younger residents stirred, but decided to delay her breakfast until they appeared.

In her youth she knew how precious the Saturday morning lie-in was, especially after a latish Friday night, and once again she had the makings of a lavish fried breakfast ready to prepare when they emerged from their cocoons.

Rosy was the first to make an appearance, although it was only to groan and shuffle along to the bathroom, and it was not until she emerged that anything could be heard from Bobbie.

When eventually they did assemble once more around the dining table, Rosy was the first to offer anything much by way of conversation.

'Remind me, Roberta, old friend, that the fruit of the apple tree has been the cause of temptation and regret since the Garden of Eden, and I really must not drink cider again.'

'Did you overdo it, girls?' asked Caroline in a suitably subdued tone.

'Somewhat, I'm afraid,' said Bobbie. 'We met up with some of the other students from the college after the film, in the pub round the corner, and it all got a bit …'

'Exuberant,' offered Rosy.

'Celebratory. It was someone's, I forget whose, but someone's birthday and he was standing drinks all round.'

'Poor Pedro,' said Rosy.

'What happened to Pedro?'

'They don't really drink pints in Spain, Caroline, and as the only lager available seemed to be that evil Stella Artois, he was soon out of his depth and swimming for the shore.'

'He was sweet though, wasn't he Rosy, singing those Spanish songs and then falling asleep like that,' said Bobbie. 'He is very pretty when he is asleep, don't you think. It's the eyelashes. And it *was* nice to meet the other people on his college course.'

'Except that he snores,' said Rosy, 'and was a bit of a dead weight for me and that David chap to lug back to his little flatlet.'

'You seemed to be getting on very well with David.'

'Passably,' said Rosy, gratefully accepting a brimming cup of coffee from Caroline and eyeing her cooked breakfast with suspicion as if it might snap at her at any moment.

'Is that all?' said Bobbie.

'Well, no, if I'm honest,' Rosy blushed. 'We exchanged telephone numbers, as it happens, and he has invited me to go and watch him play rugby next weekend'

-oo0Ooo-

Caroline had spent the previous evening sifting through her notes, taken from interviews with victims of the car scam, and the reports from a handful of freelance junior staff she employed occasionally, who had been sent to find out all they could about the world of importing cars and the legislation involved in registering a vehicle in the UK.

There was a lot of it. Particularly in regard to the complicated and long winded process imposed by the British Driver and Vehicle Licensing Centre.

To understand that, one of her freelance young reporter contacts had been sent down to their headquarters in Swansea to learn the process. He was a diligent young man and fortunately blessed with endless patience. His notes filled many pages and at first he had struggled to comprehend the fussy and pit-fall-riddled system for gaining approval to use an imported vehicle on English roads.

Caroline also had notes from discussions with local Trading Standards officers, interviewed to see if they were aware of this scam. They were inconclusive and gave her the distinct impression that she would have to present these officials with very much more solid evidence than they had so far managed to uncover on their own, before they would be prepared to interest themselves in the matter.

Amongst the notes, the most poignant story came from a middle-aged woman who she had interviewed. This woman had suffered greatly at the hands of these con artists and initially approached a local newspaper, in Woking, who had alerted Caroline to the story.

Sybil McDonald was a recently widowed housewife who, on receipt of some life insurance money, had decided to buy herself a new car.

Sybil cut a lonely figure and had taken comfort in a part-time job in a local pub where, in between pulling pints, she had heard about the possibility of importing a new car, and been impressed by how much cheaper it seemed than buying one through the more conventional route.

She had been given a website address by a drinker in the pub she had not seen before who was talking about it to an interested audience at the bar. Through that website she had soon arranged to meet a representative, who wasted no time in signing her up.

When the little Nissan arrived, it seemed fine, and she

was excited to drive it. However, it was only a few weeks later that she noticed a rattle from the engine compartment, and not being mechanically minded, or even aware of the process involved in opening the bonnet, she took it to the local main dealer.

She was astonished to receive a telephone call a little later in the day informing her that, because the car was an import and therefore not covered by a UK warranty, they could not work on it.

She was told that the dealership could not access the service history of the vehicle on their database but, by using the Vehicle Identification Number stamped into the bodywork, they had established that it was almost sixteen months old so would be outside the initial one year warranty period in any event.

Somewhat flustered, she had asked them what to do and been directed to a small independent garage who would be prepared to work on it, but she was told that she would have to pay for any repairs.

The problem, it emerged, was not major in itself, but the mechanic noticed accident damage which had been quite badly repaired around the front wing, which he recommended should be redone to a better standard. That cost more money, of course, but revealed that the car had had a life before she bought it, although the speedometer, which read in miles-per-hour, showed only a handful of miles on the counter.

Naturally. she went back to the importing company,

but was told, quite curtly, that if she referred to certain clauses in the contract she had signed, she would see that they had *not* stated that the car was new and they relied, they said, on their suppliers in Japan to check the vehicles over.

Having no spare money to engage lawyers, she went to the local newspaper, and given her reputation in such matters, the editor, who was an old friend, called Caroline to see if the story interested her.

It would take Caroline rather longer than she had initially thought to complete her investigation and she decided that she needed to ask Bobbie and Rosy if she could say for another few days.

She had found out that the importers were changing certain components on the vehicles over and above just making the speedometer read in miles-per-hour. It seemed they were also reprogramming or possibly replacing an element of the car's electronic 'brain' to reset it so that it appeared that the car had just left the factory.

Caroline was no electronics expert but she was certain that this work was going on in workshops in the UK, when these cars arrived at the docks and before they were registered for use on British roads with 'doctored' paperwork. She also had a good idea that she knew where the workshops were.

It would be easier to track down whoever was behind this scam if she was nearer the centre of things, she decided, and while she was very much looking forward to her stay there, Matravers Hall, in Wiltshire seemed too far away to be convenient, whereas from Bobbie's flat, London and the east coast ports were easily accessible.

'So would you mind,' she said, as Bobbie wiped up the breakfast things as she washed, 'if I extend my stay here for a few more days?'

'Well, that is fine as far as I'm concerned, especially if I get to help in any way,' said Bobbie. 'And I'm sure Rosy won't object, especially if you keep dishing up these fabulous breakfasts.'

'No objections from me …' came Rosy's somewhat pained voice from the lounge, were she presented a noble figure, sitting as still as she possibly could on the edge of the sofa, under a fluffy blanket. 'Just do it quietly, if you wouldn't mind, I have the headache from hell.'

-oooOoo-

Chapter 8

Caroline parked Bobbie's little sports car two roads away from her destination near the Harwich container port entrance, on the edge of the Europa Trading Estate.

As Bobbie lacked the funds to deal with it, she had paid for the mechanic to remove the sediment that was blocking the petrol pipes and get it running again, on the understanding that she could borrow it while Bobbie was at work. She had also made quite sure that there was a full tank of fuel before she set off.

Having received the car back from the garage this morning, she had wasted no time in travelling to the area around the container port where she sat now.

She checked again that her professional standard camera was ready and well concealed in the holdall in the passenger footwell and, climbed out of the little car and into a raincoat, as the inevitable drizzle began to fall.

Detective Sergeant Morris had mentioned that Linda Williams had used premises on this very industrial estate to store a large van that was impounded for having no current tax, MOT or insurance when she was last arrested, and subsequently jailed, for her involvement in a fraud importing substantial quantities of fake designer clothing and handbags, through the nearby port.

The lead was old, of course, but it was interesting to note that the premises being used for this illegal trade then were now part of a large car repair workshop that specialised in auto-electronics.

Research into that revealed that today the workshop advertised themselves as experts in reprogramming and repairing the ECU (or Engine Control Unit, sometimes called the Powertrain Control Module or PCM) which is the mysterious 'brain' of all modern cars, and needs very specialist attention if it goes wrong.

The lead, therefore, was certainly worth following. As she approached now on the other side of the road and on foot, Caroline noted with satisfaction that a grey BMW was parked outside, and a quick check with the photo stored on her mobile phone confirmed that it was the same vehicle driven by the woman calling herself "Charley Jones" to her meeting with Bobbie the previous week.

Caroline also knew that the huge container ship

currently being unloaded at the port, just down the road, had called at Malta on its way to England. and that was very significant indeed.

-ooo0oo-

'I really am most awfully sorry,' Cyril Duncan-Browne was saying as he stood in the drizzle on the doorstep of 2 Easton Drive. 'I had no idea they were storing my materials in your new garage, or I would have had a word to say about it myself.'

Geoff had no intention of inviting this annoying retired Colonel in, even if it was raining, but he had to admit that if he really knew nothing about the builders' cheek in having his materials delivered to their house, his initial fury at the man might have been misplaced.

'We very nearly sacked them, but the job is so near completion that might have been counter-productive,' he said.

'Yes, I see that,' said the Colonel attempting a lop-sided smile. 'You must have been very cross when you found out.'

'Hmm,' said Geoff and hoped that would be all.

'The confusion seems to have come about because they told me you had agreed to let them start on my project. Turns out that wasn't strictly true.'

'I never said any such thing. Quite the opposite, in fact. I got them to promise that they would not leave our job until it was finished,' stated Geoff indignantly.

'Awful mess. Awfully sorry, old man. But no hard feelings, eh? Misunderstanding quickly sorted out now, what? Oh …' Duncan-Browne was unbuttoning his coat and reaching inside, 'and I thought you might like these … sort of peace offering, if you like.'

He was holding out a paper bag with the name of the rather upmarket artisan bakery in the town emblazoned on the side.

Geoff took the bag with mumbled thanks and glancing inside, realised that it contained four magnificent and very large jam doughnuts.

'Oh! I say! That is very kind, Colo.. I mean Mr Duncan-Bro …'

'Call me Cyril.'

'Yes, well … erm, Cyril. Would you like to pop in for a cup of tea?' said Geoff clutching the precious bag and licking his lips.

-ooOOoo-

'I still no the top dollar, Bobbie. Got the rotten guts too.'

'I'm so sorry, Pedro,' said Bobbie, trying to keep the

FaceTime screen still on her iPad so as not to induce further nausea in her boyfriend.

'No drinking like that no more. How you eenglish drink so much a beer? The Pedro think he head gonna burst.'

'It was a lovely evening though, Pedro, and it was nice to meet the other students and especially the others from Spain who work with you.'

'Is nice, yays? The Teresa she look after the Pedro in the morning, make the nice coffee and buy the pastries.'

'She did seem very nice,' said Bobbie, remembering the decorative Spanish beauty with the black eyes and trim figure. 'Is she living in your house?'

'Nah, no girls allow here, remember. She living in another house over the road with a the three other girls. I going there a lot for the cooking. She furry good cook.'

'Well, that's nice,' said Bobbie, but she couldn't stop a little twinge of jealousy creeping into her thoughts.

'The Teresa she live near the Pedro in a Spain. We talk the old times. Know all same places.' Pedro chuckled. 'She the furry nice girl, too.'

Something reared up in Bobbie. All at once it occurred to her that she was a very long way away from her boyfriend and could not command the shared memories and the no-doubt easy conversation in his native language that this Teresa could. She also realised that Pedro had obviously noticed how attractive she was, and a niggling worry started to eat away at her.

'Also,' Pedro was saying, 'she say she like do the cooking for the Pedro. I furry glad. She cooking the proper Spanish paella next week. I a looking forward to that.'

'A taste of home?' The green-eyed monster that lived deep in Bobbie's otherwise blameless soul now emerged in all its revolting, destructive glory.

'Do you miss your home, Pedro,' she asked now.

'Well, not the working the hotel, but when I talking the Teresa, I missing the warm. How you eenglish stick this rain all of the time?'

A deep dread spread through Bobbie and she was unable to ignore an urge to try to compete for his affections. She thought of her own chaotic attempts at cookery, but she had to show him.
She remembered the nonsensical expressions her mother used in her ghastly books, and in particular the one about the way to a man's heart being through his stomach.

'Um, Pedro,' she found herself saying, 'How would you like to come for a proper traditional English Sunday lunch on, erm, Sunday. I could cook for you.'

It was out now, and much as she would have liked to, she could not draw the words back, especially as Pedro was enthusiastically saying that he would like that very much and how much he was looking forward to it.

'Fool!' she said under her breath.

'Que?' said Pedro.

'Oh, nothing. I was just saying not to forget to take care of yourself, Pedro.'

-ooOoo-

The drizzle was easing off a little as Caroline rounded a corner, which turned slightly away from the workshop, and discovered that there was a little 'greasy spoon' cafe with steamy windows looking towards the workshop at a slight angle.

'Perfect, just perfect. What a stroke of luck!' Caroline muttered to herself.

The smell of bacon cooking was enticing but she forced herself to walk past the cafe and round the block, back to where the little sports car was parked.

There she opened the passenger door and drew out her heavy holdall containing her camera, notebook and a few other essentials, and with a jaunty step she walked back the way she had come to arrive, this time, at the little cafe from the other direction.

She was a little dismayed to see that while she had been doing this the grey BMW, presumably containing Linda Jones, had gone. But, whilst spotting that was a bonus, it was not really what she had come to see.

This time she entered the steamy cafe, and selecting a seat by the window where there was not too much condensation on the glass, deposited her bag on the chair and went to the counter, involuntarily salivating as the smell of fried breakfast enveloped her.

-ooOoo-

Chapter 9

'I say, is that fly-fishing tackle you have got there?' said Duncan-Browne as he finished his doughnut. 'Do you fish?'

'I used to,' said Geoff, wiping the last of the sugar from his mouth on a piece of kitchen roll. 'I was pretty keen, actually, but haven't had time in recent years.'

'You have some fine tackle there, old chap. I bet that cost a pretty penny.'

Geoff had rescued his tackle from the old coal shed by the back door and had just finished cleaning it all up and sorting it out in the dining room, where they now sat.

'Not cheap, I'll admit, but unused for a very long time, I'm afraid. Do you fish?' Geoff asked.

'Oh, yes, rather. I'm the Chairman of the Byford Lakes Fishing Club as it happens. Always find me on the water there trying to catch supper for the missus.'

'Are there trout?' asked Geoff, interested.

'Plenty. Awfully well stocked now, although it was getting a trifle over- fished a couple of years ago. It is also looking a lot more picturesque now, since we had some landscaping done last winter. There is a nice little temple, I mean clubhouse, and lakes for both fly and coarse fishing there too.'

'That sounds delightful ...' and emboldened now by his description, Geoff told Duncan-Browne the story of old Mr Prentice, the gardener, and their plan to find somewhere to fly-fish to restore their shared interest in the sport.

'Well, you must come down and try our water, then!' exclaimed Duncan-Browne. 'We only allow a very limited number of guest permits each year and there is usually a waiting list, but as it happens we haven't issued this year's quota yet, so I'm sure I can get you two in as my guests, if you like.'

'Well, that is very generous, Colonel ... I mean Cyril. But is it very expensive?' Geoff was a little dubious, and although fly-fishing was always a pricy pastime, he rather suspected that the Colonel Duncan-Browne's of this world did not sully themselves fishing anywhere but on the more exclusive type of water.

'Well, put it this way, old man ...' Duncan-Browne waved away the teapot Geoff was offering to refill his cup with, 'Full membership is not something to be considered unless you are very keen, and able to justify the expense. But we are part of an Association of other fishing clubs with water all over the country, and members of the organisation that run it get a substantial discount on a few days fishing a year with us, and similar attractive arrangements on a wealth of other club's facilities.'

'That sounds interesting. How does it work?'

'From the point of view of our club, to be honest, we lose money on the deal, but they do help us in other ways. For example they gave us a grant to do some of that landscaping I was mentioning. But from the individual's point of view it is an awfully good way to get onto to fine water. I have been all over the place with them, including a spot of salmon fishing on some very exclusive estates in Scotland.'

'Now, that is something I have never done …' A glazed expression came to Geoff's face as he imagined himself hauling out a whopper.

'Yes, awfully exciting, what? But to get you started, why don't I see if I can wangle you a couple of day passes and you can see what you think of our lakes? No charge … my way of saying sorry for the mix-up over the builders.'

'But I thought the doughnuts …'

'Ah, but that was before I discovered you are a fisherman!'

-ooOoo-

Caroline considered for a moment and then, on the basis that it had to be cooked fresh, so would take longer than other items on the menu, she ordered scrambled eggs on toast with two rashers of bacon and a large size mug of strong tea.

'Hope you don't mind, but as you can see we are a bit busy at the moment. But it shouldn't take too long,' said the florid, smiling woman behind the counter.

Caroline looked around. There were four other tables occupied. Two had single occupants in Hi-Viz jackets tucking into huge plates of breakfast, and one had four similarly clad occupants eating what looked like bacon sandwiches and deep in conversation. In another corner sat a man in a suit drinking coffee. It didn't seem very busy to Caroline.

'Oh, I don't mean with them.' The large crimson faced woman indicated the other diners with a sweep of her flabby arm, 'I mean the lunches. You see we are making up the take-out lunches folk order, and the sandwiches for our van what goes round the industrial estates. Trouble is there is only me and Trudy today 'cos the other two is off with this flu what's going round. Still, if you are not in too much of a rush, take a pew and we will be with you quick as we can.'

'That is fine,' said Caroline. 'I quite understand. No rush.'

Of course she did not say so, but the longer it took the better, as far as she was concerned. She drew a novel out of her bag as she sat down, and pretended to read it.

She had a fairly good view of the workshops from where she sat, and although the windows were steamed up, there was an area by her table which seemed to be in a bit of a draught, so the grimy glass was at least partially clear. She congratulated herself again on finding this cafe, which would be so much more comfortable, and certainly warmer than sitting for an extended period in cramped conditions in the little sports car.

She did not have long to wait however before something began to happen over the road.

To one side of the workshop, there was a wide open area partially concealed behind chain-link fences and gates with tired green plastic sheets tied to the inside, no doubt to keep out prying eyes. The plastic was torn in places and flapped in the breeze, occasionally allowing glimpses of what lay within.

Caroline could make out several shipping containers which, judging by the weeds growing up around them, had been there some time, and a large fabric-sided lorry with the 'curtains' drawn back to reveal an empty interior.

Her tea was delivered and she thanked the chubby hostess with a smile.

As she watched, a large lorry drew up at the gates with a shipping container on the back and the driver got out and went into the workshop, to emerge a few moments later as unseen hands within the compound opened the gates to allow him to drive in.

With the gates open and the lorry moving inside, Caroline could see, against the back fence, a row of small, white Nissan cars, and what made them really interesting from her perspective was that none of them had number plates.

-ooOoo-

As usual, Ralph chaired the Monday morning sales meeting, but as Bobbie told Rosy later, today he seemed particularly agitated, and the meeting was interrupted.

'That horrid little creep, Elton, the production assistant, was sent in to hook Ralph out of the meeting to go to see Baldy Head, the MD.'

'Baldy Head? What an unusual name,' smiled Rosy as she stirred the casserole.

'No, his name is really Barney. To me he is Mr Head, of course, but everyone calls him Baldy behind his back because, well, he is bald.'

'I see. Well I'm glad we have got that one cleared up. What happened next?'

'We didn't know what else to do, so we went back to our desks, but we could hear Baldy Head shouting when we walked past the corridor which leads to his office.'

'Could you hear what he was saying?'

'Unfortunately not,' said Bobbie, 'but I bet it would have been good. He was giving Ralph a right old roasting, by the sound of it.'

'But I assume that is not the end of the tale, given the fact that I found you in tears when I got in from work,' Rosy looked at her friend with concern.

'Well, that is when it all kicked off. A little while later Elton came to our office and told us all to go to see Baldy in the meeting room, so we all trouped along there and sat down, wondering what to do.'

'Was Baldy, I mean Mr Head, not there then?'

'No, he came in a couple of minutes later, looking very red and cross.'

'Oh, dear.'

'Oh, dear is right. He went through the sales figures and then started to interview each of us in turn, and as it went on he got angrier and angrier. Being the most junior, he got to me last, and by then he looked ready to explode.'

'Oh, Bobbie, I'm not surprised you were in tears, then.'

'I managed to maintain a professional and dignified veneer of calm while he started in on me, but he only actually said one thing before he sent us all back to work.'

'What did he say.'

'He said, "And so we come at last to Roberta Bassington, who may be our newest recruit, but has been here quite long enough now to have something to add to these abysmal sales figures. But there is nothing, is there Roberta. Nothing at all." And with that he slapped the table and got up and left the room.'

'Oh, Lordy!'

'I honestly thought he was going to sack me on the spot, and we haven't seen Ralph since, so presumably, even though he is the owner's nephew, Baldy has found him out at last and got rid of him.'

'It must have been awful for you, Bobbie.'

'It was, and I don't think it is over yet. We each got an email before we went home saying we were to attend an individual meeting with Baldy himself at a set time on Wednesday. The email said these were to be "one-to-one" meetings and that we needed to bring our diaries and all the information about the sales leads we are working on.'

'Well, maybe you can impress him with how you have been bustling about and drumming up business ...'

'I have bustled about with determination, but the thing is, Rosy, I have absolutely nothing to show for it. Not a glimmer of interest in any of the advertising campaigns we are running from anyone I have spoken to. I've tried to get some new business and been to see everyone I can think of about what a good idea it would be to advertise on XBS Radio, but nobody wants to know. Baldy is right,' said Bobbie reaching for a tissue. 'I have nothing at all, and I really think he is going to sack me!'

-oo0Ooo-

Caroline managed to make her scrambled eggs on toast and cup of tea last long enough to see the container being unloaded, but she was not to discover what was in it as the gates were promptly closed after it entered the compound.

Having deposited its load the lorry prepared to depart and Caroline decided to act.

She hurried out of the cafe and back to where the little sports car was parked. Then she hastily arranged her camera with its long lens on the passenger seat and drove around the corner with the windows open.

As the lorry came out of the gates she grabbed her camera and took what pictures she could whilst driving as slowly as she dared, with one hand, as the gates were once again closed by unseen hands.

The lorry, now in front of her, turned back towards the port, and she drove past the little cafe, round the corner, and stopped to briefly examine her photographs.

As she put the camera back in its holdall she was shocked when someone tapped on the driver's side window.

She scrabbled to select first gear with the intention of driving off rapidly, but abandoned the attempt when a Police Identification Card was pressed against the window, and its owner started to open the door.

'Sorry to make you jump. Caroline Bassington, isn't it?'

It was the man in the suit from the cafe and he was smiling.

'DS Morris said you might pop by and take a look at this place. We have been keeping an eye on it for a couple of days now.'

'Gosh, you made me jump!' said Caroline, struggling to catch her breath.

'Sorry about that, but I couldn't really make myself known to you inside the cafe. My name is Phelps, Detective Constable Shaun Phelps. I'm just filling in really on this one, as we have so many officers off with this flu that is doing the rounds. Did you get any decent pictures?'

Caroline unwound herself from the little car and stood up.

'Sorry I gave you a turn,' DC Phelps was holding out his hand. 'Nice to meet you. You are something of a celebrity back at The Yard.'

-oooOoo-

Chapter 10

At last the builders had finished.

Janet and Geoff had employed Derek, Mr Prentice the gardener's grandson, to paint the new utility room and that efficient young man had made an excellent job of it, and now, late in the day as he was beginning to lose the light, he was completing the laying a cinder path along the side of the new garage.

'Grandad will want to park his bike here, no doubt,' he explained, 'so I've made it a bit wider just here so you can get round.'

'That is very thoughtful of you,' said Janet. 'And you are right. Your grandfather left his bicycle beside the old garage for as long as I can remember, and will no doubt continue to do the same now we have this new one.'

'I have to say it does look good.' Geoff, standing on the lawn halfway down the garden, was looking back at the new extension as Janet joined him.

'Yes, it does, doesn't it. I wonder how Mr Duncan-Browne is getting on with the builders now. I can't say I'm not pleased to see the back of them,' she said.

'He is dreading his mother-in-law moving in, he told me. She bullies him unmercifully, apparently.'

'Horrible woman. I hope we don't have to see her.' Janet linked her arm with his and led him towards the house. 'Come on, it's getting cold and I want to discuss the choice of new washing machines with you.'

'Right,' said Geoff. He had been very happy helping Janet make her selections of all the new things they were buying, and felt much better now that he was funding the modernisations, which made him feel that at last he was pulling his weight financially.

'And also,' Janet was saying, 'I want to go over the wedding plans again, if you can bear it. I'm starting to get nervous about that.'

But all that would have to wait as Bobbie's little sports car pulled into the drive with her characteristic shower of gravel. She was not expected, and whilst Janet smiled in happy anticipation of seeing her, Geoff could not help wondering why she had chosen to arrive unannounced.

-oooOoo-

It was early evening by the time Caroline got back to

the flat and Rosy was already cooking the dinner.

Bobbie was anxious to use the little sports car and it fell to Rosy to explain how she had found Bobbie crying when she got home from work.

Caroline was very concerned to hear that her favourite niece was having a tough time at work and resolved to discuss it with her when she returned, if she made it, as she had promised, in time for supper.

At Geoff and Janet's house, Bobbie was fighting back tears once again.

'And because I'm so useless, never mind that I'm the latest person to join, it's going to be me that gets the sack …' she was saying.

'How much does it cost to advertise on the radio?' asked Janet as an idea started to form in her mind.

'Well, that is half the problem. It is really expensive, and you have to take out a rolling series of adverts, they won't sell just one, otherwise I might have had a bit more luck selling them.'

'Now, come on, Bobbie. Let's think this through,' said Geoff. 'You say you have contacted everyone you can think of to try to sell them advertising?'

'Yes, Uncle Geoff. And I know what you are thinking, don't think I don't appreciate it, Janet, but dentists don't need to advertise. You said yourself that your books are full and you have a waiting list.'

'I'm afraid that is true, Bobbie. It was a rather silly idea. I'm just trying to think of things to help you.' Janet was squeezing her arm gently.

'Thank you, it is sweet of you, Janet.' Bobbie dried her eyes. 'But I actually think it is too late now. It takes weeks to get an ad. recorded and edited after the contract is signed, and because so many customers pull out half way through, we don't get paid on it until it goes on the air. So even if I sold something today I couldn't count it as a sale.'

'And you are sure you have done all you can to correct the situation?' Geoff asked.

'I've been flogging my guts out, if you will excuse the indelicate allusion, but as Baldy said, I've got nothing. And it's not just me. The other reps are doing really badly too. We have this policy of selling repeats, that is a run of adverts rather than singles or short runs, so it makes us uncompetitive and a big financial commitment for the clients. They don't like it and it is very difficult to get even a glimmer of interest.'

'Well, why doesn't the company change the policy?' Janet asked, reasonably enough.

'It is the owner who won't hear of that. Ralph's uncle. He says that is how they have sold advertising in the past and the company is respected for retaining its longstanding customers with rolling advertising contracts. That is what he wants us to secure, but as a local radio station we don't deal with companies who can take on that sort of financial commitment. All of those big boys already advertise with us and we are scrabbling about trying to find the crumbs dropped from their table in the form of little local companies with limited cash-flow and lacking their deep pockets.'

'In that case,' said Geoff, 'if the bosses won't face those realities, it sounds as though you are on a hiding to nothing.'

'Oh, Uncle Geoff, what am I going to do?' Bobbie reached for the tissues in the box Janet had strategically placed at her elbow. 'How am I going to pay the bills and the rent if I lose my job?'

'Well, you could always move in ...'

'No, Janet, we don't need to be thinking like that,' interrupted Geoff. 'It is *not* going to come to that.'

'But ...'

'I suggest that when you go to this meeting on Wednesday, you have in your pocket your resignation already typed out, so that if you are threatened with the sack you can resign first.' Geoff took Bobbie's hand as she let out a little hiccup of dismay. 'Nothing looks worse on the C.V. of a young person just starting out than getting the sack from their first job. If you resign it shows you in a different light. It demonstrates that you can think things through. Even if the job was wrong for you, if you resign then you get the chance to explain why to new prospective employers without making it obvious that you were not very good at it.'

'I see what you mean, Geoff,' said Janet. 'That makes sense.'

'And you don't have to produce the letter if the interview doesn't go as you suspect it might. It is just an insurance policy.'

'Uncle Geoff …'

'Now, let's have a look in the local paper. I've got it here. Let's see what other jobs there are out there that would suit a young lady of your obvious charm and good sense. Look, I see Marshalls the Jewellers are advertising for staff to present their "superior new ranges", and here, Debenhams are advertising for staff in their hat department …'

'Selling hats! Me?'

'Or there is a job here for a trainee riveter in a steam engine restoration yard …'

Bobbie smiled at last. 'Oh, Uncle Geoff, you are a wonder. And you are right; even if I end up selling nails in the ironmongers under the flat, I should be able to find something …'

'Of course you will. Now shall we go and type up that letter and print it off, just in case?'

-ooo0oo-

Rosy's casserole was delicious and even Bobbie enjoyed it, now that she had a firm plan in mind as to how to handle matters back in the office.

Caroline had discussed the situation with her at some length and offered a shoulder to cry on if she needed it.

Rosy too, had been supportive although her offer to "chuck this Baldy Head out of the window to see if he bounces," was perhaps not entirely helpful.

After a brief and none too satisfactory 'FaceTime' chat with Pedro, during which she decided not to mention her problems, and just listened as he explained how he and Teresa had been shopping for the ingredients of the paella she was planning, she retired early to bed.

Inevitably, Bobbie slept fitfully, and Tuesday dawned with all the old fears pressing on her mind as much as ever, but at least she had a plan now, and a surreptitious scan of the newspapers in the office did reveal that there were jobs being advertised if she did need to find a new one.

By the time she returned to the flat that evening she was in a much better frame of mind, having decided that what would be, would be.

-oo0Ooo-

Caroline put her notebook away and leaned back on

the sofa to take stock.

DS Morris had had the photos she took by email and DC Phelps, whom she met outside the little cafe in Harwich, had filled him in on what they saw. But she still needed more. The strings were not tying together quite yet. But how to do it?

If only she could get hold of one of these cars and get an expert to look at it to discover how it was made to appear to be a new car. She needed something physical.

She had the recording of Linda Jones, posing as Charley Williams and stating that these cars were new, but that was not going to be enough to shut down this operation, and the company could just claim it was a rogue salesman, pretend to sack her, and that would be that.

No. What was needed was some hard evidence that the cars had been tampered with in some way, in a deliberate attempt to mislead, by giving the impression that they were brand new.

And why, when it came to registering them in the UK, didn't the date stamp within the V.I.N. number alert the British authorities to the fact that the car had had a life before coming to these shores. How was that done?

Caroline reached into her bag and scrolled through the photographs on her camera. The evidence was there somewhere, if she could only get her hands on it.

-ooOoo-

As she arrived for work on Wednesday, Bobbie was surprised to find the office half empty.

The desk in Ralph's little office had been cleared, so it was pretty obvious that he wasn't coming back, and the other reps who were in, looked gaunt and troubled.

There was nobody in the production department, and the only normal bustling activity was in the studio where the music radio show was being broadcast as usual by the middle-aged, adenoidal, troglodyte that passed for a morning DJ.

As she made herself a coffee Bobbie gave an involuntary shudder as it occurred to her that the radio station, not just the sales team, was in trouble.

The spotty youth, Elton, was passing from office to office and she noticed that everyone seemed to be heading for the meeting room. When Elton arrived at the sales office he told those present that they were to join the throng there immediately and Bobbie followed him along the corridor.

'What's happening, Elton?' She asked his disappearing back, and he stopped in his tracks and turned to face her.

His eyes were red and he reached into his pocket for

his handkerchief and blew his nose before he spoke.

'I'm sorry, Bobbie. We will find out all about it in a minute, but XBS Radio has gone bust.'

-oo0Ooo-

Chapter 11

Fishing, as anyone who indulges in the piscatorial pastime will tell you, is an imprecise art and success is affected by many factors beyond the fisherman's control.

Perversely the fish are often more active and likely to take the bait when it is raining and cold, which is unpleasant for the fisherman, but seems to encourage the fish. Today the weather was glorious and Colonel Duncan-Browne, Geoff and old Mr Prentice arranged their tackle on the green and healthy-looking grass in a shaft of golden sunlight after a pleasant drive to the lakes, during which Mr Prentice resisted the urge to smoke, in the Colonel's smart estate car.

All of nature smiled on the three intrepid sportsmen who, ignoring for a moment the wonderful display of wild flowers in joyful bloom, the cheerful song of the birds and the comforting warmth of the early morning sun, looked at the still water of the lake before them in dismay.

'Not a sign,' said Mr Prentice, or Billy, to the assembled group.

'Maybe if we try a little further round by those trees,' suggested Geoff.

'Too shallow there, I'm afraid,' said the Colonel. 'And there is more tangled tackle in those trees than leaves. That stretch won't be any good until the river is in spate and the water level rises.'

'What d'you suggest?' Billy Prentice asked, lighting a cigarette.

'We could try where the river enters the lake. It is a bit rocky and we will have to wade in a bit, but it might yield something.'

So the three gathered up their tackle and, noticing for the first time the cloudless blue sky, they trudged round to the spot indicated and fought their way disconsolately through the luxuriant undergrowth, and profusely flowering bushes; batting aside bees, dragonflies, beetles, and colourful butterflies, to a spot where they could struggle into their waders and take to the flowing water.

-oo0Ooo-

Of course it was so obvious, now that she thought about it, and as long as Sybil McDonald didn't mind, the solution was soon going to be at hand.

Gary, Geoff's tame mechanic and the only person entrusted to touch her brother-in-law Geoff's precious Jaguar was, he said, quite prepared to help.

'Few can git the car ta me, Oi can git my mate ta 'ave a lookatit, no bother,' he said, and had gone on to explain that whilst he was no expert in the mysterious world of auto-electronics, he knew a young man who understood that sort of thing and was bound to be able to help.

''Lo?' said Sybil McDonald, yawning and trying to shake the fuzziness of a late night from her head as she answered the telephone.

'Sybil?' said Caroline. 'It's Caroline Bassington here, you remember we met to discuss your car … look, I'm sorry to trouble you, but …'

''S no trouble. Hello Caroline. 'Scuse me, I've just woken up.'

'Oh, I didn't mean to disturb you …'

'S fine. We barmaids have to keep odd hours. Long night, I'm afraid. Now what can I do for you?'

Caroline took a deep breath and started to set out her plan.

-oooOoo-

With the customary shower of gravel, Bobbie's little

sports car arrived on Geoff and Janet's drive.

Geoff, who had only been back from his fishing trip for a few minutes, was startled by the noise and was not expecting visitors, so he hurried to the front door just as Bobbie was approaching it.

'Bobbie! Whatever are you doing here at this hour?'

Bobbie's tear stained face told him immediately that it was not good news, and without another word he wrapped her in his arms.

'Un… Un… Uncle Geoff,' sobbed Bobbie.

'All right, poppet. Come in and tell me all about it.'

It took a while, but several tissues and a half a cup of hot, sweet tea later, Bobbie managed to get the story out, and reaching into the pocket of her jacket drew out the crumpled letter she had been given which set out the terms of her redundancy.

'Well,' said Geoff, with a boisterousness he did not feel, 'in a way this is excellent news. At least you didn't get the sack, and any future employer cannot blame you for being made redundant if the company went under.'

'But what am I going to do, Uncle Geoff! I owe Rosy money as it is … and … and …'

'Now let's try to think this through.' Geoff was remembering the old days when Bobbie, returning from school after some calamity, ran to him for calm counsel and together they plotted a way out of her difficulties. 'I've got my pad and a pen here: let's make a list of where we are.'

-oo0Ooo-

'So, do we have trout for supper?' Janet closed the front door and looked at Geoff expectantly.

'Er, no,' said Geoff sheepishly. 'Not so much as a bite all day.'

'Oh, dear,' chuckled Janet. 'So there is nothing for tea?'

'You weren't depending …'

'No, of course not, you silly clot. There is that cold chicken.' Janet flashed one of her illuminating smiles that bathed Geoff in light. 'So was the fishing a complete wash out?'

'On the contrary. We had a wonderful day and the weather was lovely, as was the setting.'

'But you didn't catch any fish. I thought that was the whole point …'

'I'll admit that catching fish would have been nice, but that is not all there is to fishing … being out in the fresh air, in the countryside is a great pleasure too,' Geoff explained.

'Pretty expensive way of getting a breath of fresh air, if you ask me.'

Geoff, seeing he had some more work to do to get Janet to see the attraction of his chosen sport, decided to prepare the ground.

'You sit down while I make a cup of tea, love, then I will explain. There is something else I have to tell you as well'

-ooOoo-

Chapter 12

Caroline read Bobbie's redundancy letter again and tried to get her thoughts in order.

Bobbie had explained that Geoff would pay her rent this month and cover the outstanding electricity bill as well as her unpaid contributions due to Rosy for shopping, so that she had a clean sheet for now. But understandably Bobbie was panicking rather about the immediate future.

Rosy had been marvellous, initially trying to get Bobbie to accept her offer to forget about what she was owed and then, finally accepting Geoff's generous contribution, gently going through the budget Geoff had helped Bobbie prepare to see where economies could be made, whilst all the time reassuring her that a new and better job was just around the corner.

Laying the letter aside, Caroline made a decision and went to see Bobbie in her bedroom.

Bobbie was laying out clothes on the bed.

'What are you doing?' Caroline asked.

'I'm working out which clothes I can sell,' she said. 'Do you think I will get much for the sports car?'

Caroline was very fond of Bobbie and this bought a lump to her throat.

'Put all that back in your wardrobe, Bobbie,' she said. 'You won't need to sell anything if you agree to what I have to propose.'

'What do you mean, Auntie Caroline? This is all I have, and the only way I can raise some money.'

'Not if you accept a new job.'

'Who is going to offer a loser like *me* a new job, especially one that will pay up in time to cover the next shopping do and the rent?' Bobbie sat down hard on the bed amongst the piles of clothes.

'I am,' said Caroline.

'Pardon?' Bobbie looked at her aunt questioningly.

'I said I am. I am going to offer you a job, if you want it. Would you like to hear a bit more about it?'

Bobbie, who was sitting now with her mouth open, could only manage an astonished nod as she hitched up her jaw.

-oo0Ooo-

'So what started out as the blackest day of my young life has turned out to be a joyful cause for celebration.'

It was no good. Bobbie just couldn't keep still and although Pedro complained that it made the FaceTime picture go fuzzy, she was dancing round the room on the tips of her toes in excitement.

'Is furry good, Bobbie. You auntie, you say she the hot shot newshound and a soon you be too. Be on the telly and everything!'

'Well, I don't know about that. And to start with, until we sell some stories, I'm going to be a bit short of money because she can only afford to pay me the equivalent of my basic salary at the radio station. But it is a much more exciting job, and I'm sure that managing the London office of her business will be fun.'

'You the manager, Bobbie?'

'Well, no, not really, I just made that bit up. But I will be the only employee in London and the suburbs, so that is kind of the same thing. Most of the time I will be going where Aunt Caroline tells me and doing as I'm told. Actually,' said Bobbie pausing for breath, 'I'm not actually sure what I will be doing. So far all I know is I have to go to Woking on the train and pick up a car, and then take it to Gary, the mechanic, round the corner from here.'

'Is better than the selling the radio you no good at.'

'Yes, well thanks for reminding me about that. How was your paella with Teresa and the other students?'

'Oh, yays! Is furry nice. I having the three plates!'

'Did the other students like it?'

'Other? ... No, the Teresa cook it up just a for me. She furry nice girl, I liking, so the Pedro he do all the washing up!'

'So it was just you and Teresa? Nobody else was there?'

'No, just a we ...'

'Oh,' said Bobbie, and there was a longish pause.

'Look, I have to go now, Pedro. ... Call me tomorrow ... if you want to ... If you are not too busy with Teresa.'

-oo0Ooo-

Geoff knew that the Wiltshire Bassingtons (as opposed to the Kent Bassingtons, or, heaven forfend, the Shropshire Bassingtons) had a reputation as doers rather than talkers. He had married into the family, after all.

Although his ex-wife had Bassingtons as in-laws, in the form of Bobbie Bassington's mother and father, he had seen quite enough of that side of the family to form a well-rounded impression of their family traits.

Caroline, for example, had a determined, no-nonsense attitude to life and getting things done. Nothing seemed to faze her, and when she set her mind to something it would take a considerable amount of explosive to distract her from her chosen course.

Such it was with this issue of offering Bobbie a job.

Geoff asked if her business could afford a full time employee, and received a look which, not only told him to mind his own business, but made him shrink like a dying mushroom.

He tried again, once he had recovered, by taking a different tack and asking if Bobbie was the right sort of person for a career at the sharper end of journalism.

This Caroline rebuffed, by saying imperiously,'Roberta is her father's daughter, and where a lesser man would think twice about the challenges of the life of an investigative journalist, he was a Bassington, and as he always said, Bassingtons are *not* lesser men. That spirit,' she said, 'runs in the blood of the female Bassingtons too, especially the Wiltshire Bassingtons!'

She went on to remind Geoff, at some length, that various generations of this ancient family had distinguished themselves in military combat, politics and a bewildering array of other fields of endeavour, citing her examples with such rapidity that Geoff struggled to keep up with her.

When she finally ran down and sat glowering at him in the middle of the sofa like some miniature, malevolent, island volcano, daring him to start something, all he could think to say was, 'Would you like another cup of tea, Caroline?'

-ooOoo-

Chapter 13

'I'm sure it is all just a misunderstanding,' said Janet, passing Bobbie the tea towel as she started to wash up. 'Perhaps Pedro didn't understand what you were asking.'

'I'd love to think you were right, Janet, but he clearly stated that this Teresa cooked the paella just for him and there was nobody else there.'

'Well, perhaps they all had lectures to go to …'

'No. We have to face the facts. Teresa with her expressive black eyes, gorgeous tan and bigger boobs than mine, is making a play for Pedro, and it seems he is lapping it up.'

'Lapping it up?'

'Just as he lapped up three plates of her loathsome underhanded cooking.'

'I'm sure it is not like that at all …'

'And it was only last week that he told me he loved me.' Bobbie set the tea towel down and sank into a kitchen chair.

'It is my own fault. Well, mother's fault actually. She sent me to this strict private school run by nuns, you see.'

'I see,' said Janet, who didn't see at all, but wanted to demonstrate sisterly support.

'They force-fed us all this guff about hell-fire and damnation awaiting girls who let boys … you know, and how we had to save ourselves. It has always haunted me. I've got a more balanced view of all that religious stuff now, of course, but the wounds those nuns inflicted run deep. Perhaps if I had jumped into bed with Pedro at the first opportunity none of this would have happened.'

'Oh, I'm sure Pedro doesn't …'

'I rather suspect he does. Or at least wants to. With the undeniably pretty poisonous pustule of paella-plate-passing perfection that is the pneumatic Teresa.'

-ooOoo-

Rosy was confused.

Now that Bobbie's precarious finances had been put on a firmer footing and her debts repaid, she thought she would be pleased when she suggested that they could go and buy the ingredients together for the traditional English roast dinner which she had offered to cook on Sunday.

Bobbie's rather tart refusal came as a shock, and as it was obvious that she didn't want to talk about it, she left it at that. She knew that Bobbie regretted that she had offered to cook, but when they previously discussed it, and Caroline offered to help, she seemed a little happier about it. What had bought on this sudden change was a mystery.

That did not mean that the surprise Rosy was planning wasn't still on, though, and she smiled at the thought of her plans coming together.

The chance to celebrate Bobbie's new job as well would also add that little bit extra to the proceedings and cheer everyone up, and she was very much looking forward to it.

She was convinced that Bobbie knew nothing about what was being planned, and what with one thing and another, hadn't given her upcoming birthday any thought at all.

-oooOoo-

'Hola, Bobbie,' chirped Pedro as the FaceTime call connected. 'Look this!'

Pedro was trying to hold his phone in one hand and what looked like a slightly out of focus blue cloud in the other.

'You know I keep a saying needing the new jeans, well now I got! We go in the Teresa car to the mall and a chose these.'

'Oh,' said Bobbie.

'Teresa she got the car now, her dad buying. He working the same bank as we, but he high up top manager got plenty money. No easy parking round here but he buy her the special parking permit too. Maybe going the Richmond Park next a week for a drive to try out.'

'Oh,' said Bobbie.

'Yays. The Teresa, she always got the fun ideas.'

'Erm …' said Bobbie.

'I got the new … um … Teresa,' he called over his shoulder. 'What called is this, please? … Oh, yes. Got new scarf keep the Pedro neck warm in the winter too.'

'Is Teresa there with you?'

'Yays, I in her house, got the better broadband here, see. Also there is a garden so we been sunbathing. I staying here many times. Is much nicer stay here than my studio.'

'Oh,' said Bobbie.

'Tonight is a live music and disco at the Estudant

Union . Teresa, she got the tickets so we going together in the car.'

There was a silence.

'Bobbie?'

'About Sunday lunch, Pedro. That's all off now. You will probably prefer to go for a nice romantic drive in the park with Teresa anyway, so … so I don't think there is any point in us going on, do you? It seems you are having plenty of fun with Teresa and you obviously enjoy being with her all the time, so … so … if that is what you want then maybe we should … well, if you like being with her so much then … then … oh, goodbye, Pedro.'

And she cut the connection and turned her iPad off.

-oo0Ooo-

Cyril Duncan-Browne had happened to arrive at 2 Easton Drive just as old Billy Prentice drew up on his bicycle.

''Ullo, there, Colonel,' he said, touching the peak of the smarter of his two caps. 'Come to see Geoff?'

'Hello, old chap. Yes, I thought you two might like these,' and he held out two day passes for Byford Lakes fishing club.

'Coo!' said Billy. 'Day passes! Tha's triffik!'

'Yes, well, be that as it may, Billy,' Duncan-Browne glanced furtively at the front door of 2 Easton Drive. 'I've been meaning to have a word with you about some gardening work. Would you be interested in coming to work for the wife and me, and helping us sort the garden out when the building work to the extension is finished? ... Payment in cash, of course.'

-ooo0oo-

On the train to Woking, Bobbie stared blankly out of the window. It was hot and sultry, but she barely noticed.

Pedro had tried several times to call her mobile phone this morning, but she had blocked his number so he couldn't even leave a voice message. He had just sent his twenty-third email but she had diverted them all to the 'Junk' file and hadn't opened any of them. As soon as she found out how to do it, she would block his emails too, she decided.

She was surprised that she hadn't cried, but put it down to anger.
Now she just felt empty.

She looked again at the little piece of paper with the address her Aunt Caroline had written down for her and read the post-script at the bottom where her aunt had noted that she must drive slowly and carefully.

She thought she should be excited as this was the first

day of her new job, but she could not seem to move on from the knot of grief and anger that had robbed her of sleep and left her drained and exhausted.

As the train pulled into the station she shook herself and took in her surroundings properly for the first time. She needed to find the taxi rank and felt in her handbag again to make sure the 'expenses money' she had been given was safely tucked away.

There was a helpful sign pointing to the taxi rank just inside the station entrance, but, when she got there, no taxis were in sight.

Another helpful sign attached to a lamppost advised her that 'Chekker Cabs' could be contacted by calling the number shown, and in the absence of any actual taxis, she dialled the number and listened to the phone ringing.

'Yus?' said a voice.

'Is that Chekker Cabs?'

'Yus. Ow ken oi be hov assistance?'

And Bobbie explained where she was and where she wanted to go.

'Give it five mins, ducky,' said the voice and hung up.

Another helpful sign informed Bobbie that the wooden bench she was sitting on was placed there in memory of 'Stationmaster Alf Dobbins, much-loved husband of Dolly and sons Augustus and Algernon.'

She smiled at the pretentious children's names and wondered if they were teased at school, as with a roar and a rattle, an elderly Ford with a black bonnet, doors and boot, contrasting with the otherwise-white paintwork, screeched to a halt alongside her, and the driver called through the open window.

'Dew call Chekker Cabs, Miss? Hop in then!

It was only a short drive to 'The Crown and Anchor' public house, but the driver pressed a card into her hand as she paid and said, 'Few need a cab again, you call Chekker Cabs, sweetie, and ask for me. Name's Gus Dobbins.'

And with that he was gone.

-oo0oo-

Chapter 14

As Rosy finished the call and thanked David for making her aware of the situation, she remembered to ask him if the rugby match he was playing in on Sunday was still going ahead and breathlessly reminded him that he had asked her to come along.

She was relieved when he confirmed that he was looking forward to seeing her again and he suggested they went for a meal afterwards. This time, Rosy thought, it really is a date.

As she hung up, the doorbell rang, and she accepted a huge bouquet of flowers on Bobbie's behalf.

The meaning on the little card attached was plain enough and she read,
'Please, Bobbie, what I do? I really love you. Pedro.'

-ooOOoo-

The Crown and Anchor was a fairly typical Victorian

pub except that, for some inexplicable reason, the landlord had taken it into his head to paint the exterior bright blue. Other than that it looked welcoming enough and Bobbie stepped through the door with confidence.

There was a bar facing her, with a few early drinkers in one corner taking their ease, and a short woman with green hair polishing the beer pumps at the far end of the bar counter.

'Hello,' said Bobbie, approaching her, 'I'm looking for Sybil McDonald.'

'And you have found her,' smiled the woman 'Would you be Caroline's niece?'

Bobbie was rather hoping to introduce herself as Caroline's assistant, but there was no getting away from the accuracy of the title Sybil gave her, so she admitted that she was indeed her niece.

'The car is in the car park. Come on, I'll show you,' and calling to some unseen person in a back room to keep an eye on the bar, she extracted some keys from her pocket and directed Bobbie to the door through which she had come.

The car was sitting in the full sun and a blast of hot air hit them as they opened the door.

'Blimey, it's hot today!' exclaimed Sybil. 'Let's open the doors and windows and let it cool down a bit!'

The little car was bright white and perfectly clean, and it was obviously Sybil's pride and joy. Bobbie noticed that she had personalised it with a few little touches.

The fluffy cushion on the back seat and the collection of soft toys on the back shelf caught her eye, as did the two air-fresheners and the little teddy bear hanging from the rear view mirror. Rosy would tease her if she saw Bobbie driving this, she thought.

As the car cooled Sybil pointed out the controls and when Bobbie asked the best route back to the main road, she gave clear directions in a businesslike way.

'I used to be a taxi driver, so I know all the routes round here,' she offered.

'Have you lived here long?' asked Bobbie conversationally.

'All my life. I was born in a little house two roads over, christened and married in the church you see over there, and for my sins I will probably be buried there too. Boring, aren't I.'

'Not at all,' said Bobbie 'It seems a nice area to live in, so who can blame you for staying put.'

'Nice area? Well, yes, I suppose it is not too bad, but my great joy is getting away from it on cruise ships. I have been on cruises all over the world, pretty much. My husband, rest his soul, was in the Merchant Navy, so he had itchy feet, you might say, and we spent every penny we had on travel.'

With a sigh, Sybil turned away.

"Course that's all history now. I can't afford to do that no more. I wouldn't have been able to buy this car if not for a bit of life insurance money, and now I wish I still had that in the bank.'

Bobbie was at a loss as to what to say at this point.

'Look, I had better get back in. Are you all right driving the car?'

'I'll be fine,' said Bobbie, accepting the keys she was offering.

'It has only got a tiddly little engine and don't like going up hills so much, and it takes a while to build up speed, so have patience with it.'

'No problem,' said Bobbie. 'I shall be very careful.'

-oo0Ooo-

Sybil's directions to the main road were easy to follow and Bobbie was soon on her way.

She had noticed that the car's engine made a lot of noise for very little action, and it was certainly no sports car, but it got along well enough and they were soon in stop-start traffic where performance was hardly an issue.

Before driving off Bobbie had spent some time

adjusting the seat for her taller frame and all the mirrors to get them right, and it was just as well that she did.

About twenty minutes into the journey, as the traffic started to move and they approached a roundabout coming from a two-lane section of road, Bobbie caught the merest glimpse in her door mirror of a white van driving up fast alongside, and much too close.

It was veering towards her and accelerating in the outside lane, and Bobbie had to take avoiding action by pulling hard to the left.

The van swerved into the lane in front of her and its slightly open back doors, tied almost shut with string, missed her front wing by millimetres and then, for some inexplicable reason, it braked sharply.

The van was so close that Bobbie's only option was to veer off the roundabout taking the left-hand exit, otherwise a collision was inevitable. She found herself groping for the horn which, on this little car, was not in the middle of the steering wheel.

As she fought to gain control, she found she had been forced to turn into a side road off the roundabout, and she was in a wide avenue with little parades of shops on each side.

-oo0Ooo-

'It's all fixed up,' said Gary 'Can you get the car here by half four? My mate Algy should be here by then.'

'No problem,' said Bobbie, 'I'll be there.'

Gary (Geoff's preferred mechanic, and the only person trusted to look after his Jaguar) had called in an expert to take a look at Sybil's car and try to work out how it had been tampered with.

Standing about in Gary's grimy workshop while these two scratched their heads was not really Bobbie's idea of fun but she supposed investigative journalists had to take the rough with the smooth in order to get a scoop.

To get her breath back, after the heart-stopping moment with the white van, she had parked for a while outside some shops, and when she felt herself again, had called into a Post Office and stationers. There she had bought a notebook, very much in the style of the one her Aunt Caroline used.

As she clipped a pen to the ring binding she regarded it as one of the tools of her trade and decided it would always be with her.
Investigative journalists had to be prepared. Who knew when a story would present itself?

Gary was all right, but he *was* a bit leery, so back at the flat, she changed out of her cool, short summer dress into jeans, although the sun was still quite hot.

As she pulled her jeans on she became aware that something was in the pocket and, rooting it out, she found, to her horror, that it was the emergency button Caroline had given her in the 'safe house' in Kensington. The gadget belonged there and she had forgotten to leave it as she made her hasty departure.

Bobbie chewed her lip.

When she had to tell Caroline that she had made her first mistake in her new job already, she wondered if she was about to face unemployment once again.

-ooOoo-

Bobbie drove slowly and carefully to Gary's workshop, and as she climbed out of Sybil's little car and closed the door, a loud and snarling old Ford drew into the yard.

This odd car was basically black, but had a white bonnet, doors and boot and made a noise more like a racing car than a family saloon.

Killing the growling engine, an athletic-looking young man jumped out, and seeing Gary coming out of the workshop, called out to him.

'Gazza! Hello, mate ! Nice to see you again!'

As Gary shook his hand he noticed Bobbie for the first time.

'Well, hullo! And who do we have here, then? Gazza, you kept this young beauty quiet …'

Moving towards her with his hand held out in greeting, he said 'Algy Dobbins, extremely talented tuner and auto-electrician at your service, and you are?'

''Ullo Algy,' chuckled Gary. 'Still as big-headed as ever, I see! This is Bobbie. Nah play nice, please. Miss Bobbie is the niece of one of my favourite customers, so watch it!'

'How do you do?' said Bobbie, and glancing again at the idiosyncratic car, she realised who this was.

'Are you Algernon Dobbins, younger son of the late Alf Dobbins, former Stationmaster at Woking railway station and brother to Augustus Dobbins, of Chekker Cabs?'

'Blimey!' said Algy and Gary in unison.

'How did you know all that?' asked Algy.

'I'm training to be an investigative journalist,' said Bobbie. 'We have to notice every little detail.'

She did eventually own up to how she had done it, but, being Bobbie, she enjoyed her few moments of mystique as she baffled her audience.

-ooOoo-

Chapter 15

Detective Sergeant Morris passed Caroline a polystyrene cup of something lukewarm and brown as the interview room door opened and the prisoner shuffled in.

'Sorry, you'll have to wait outside, Caroline,' said DS Morris, 'but I shan't be very long.'

'No problem,' said Caroline, resuming her seat in the visitors' waiting area.

'Sit down, please,' said the warden, closing the door. 'This is Anne Susan Simmons, Detective Sergeant Morris. I shall be just outside the door if you need me,' and she stepped into a small vestibule with a couple of plastic chairs and a wired glass panel looking into the interview room.

'Hello again, Anne,' said DS Morris. 'Long time no see.'

'Not 'arf long enough for me,' smirked the prisoner.

'Probably not, but I don't want to cut into your busy

day, so I'll come straight to the point. When you shared a cell with Linda Williams did she say anything about importing cars?'

'What if she did?'

'I notice that your parole is coming up next month, Anne...'

'Don't you balls that up for me! Oi've been as good as gold in 'ere and dun me time quiet, like.'

'So, returning to the subject of importing cars, what did Linda say about it?'

'Nuffink.'

'Oh, come now, Anne. We know she is renting that workshop in Harwich from your brother-in-law again, just as she did when she was caught importing fake designer handbags. Pays in cash, does she?'

-ooo0oo-

'It's just an off-the-shelf Chinese replacement ECU,' Algy was saying. 'No, hang on, what's this?'

Using his mobile phone as a torch, Algy was looking at the boxes containing the electronics in the engine compartment of Sybil's little car, as Gary and Bobbie looked on.

'This box has been opened. The seams have been split and then the plastic welded up again, by the looks of it. Very interesting. Can I take it out and put it on my tester?'

'Erm … Well, your auntie did say not to do any damage, like, didn't she, Bobbie' Gary looked uncomfortable.

'Oh, that's all right, you will never know I've been here and I'll attach my special homemade shunt first so the car's settings will be unaltered. It's an advanced form of the car tuner's favourite tool, and of my own design.'

'Or roight, if you're sure, but be ever so careful. That's a brand new car an' we don't want to do no damage'

'Well,' said Bobbie, 'I guess it wouldn't do any harm …' and she explained how they believed the car's age had been disguised before it was sold as a new car.

'Well, you wouldn't change the ECU on a brand new car unless something was seriously wrong, and certainly not for a cheap Chinese after-market one like this… that's very interesting, but this is not just a swap,' said Algy, straightening up. 'This box has been tampered with.'

The boot of Algy's car, when he opened it, contained what looked like the immense mixing desk in the radio studio where she had worked. Bobbie looked at the twinkling lights, screens, and myriad of sliding and rotary controls in awe as Algy reached in and drew out one end of a thick shank of wire. He lifted a small computer screen out and positioned it on the black and white car's roof so that he could see it while working under Sybil's bonnet.

-oo0Ooo-

Geoff wondered if Janet would accuse him of buying it from a fishmonger's on the way home.

But there it sat, on an oval plate in the fridge, now cleaned and gutted. It was quite the most beautiful trout Geoff had ever seen. Billy Prentice had one too, and both had had a marvellous and successful day, fishing at Byford Lakes.

Geoff had telephoned Colonel Cyril Duncan-Browne to thank him for the day tickets and to enthuse about their success, after he dropped Billy home.

Billy, without being asked of course, had refrained from smoking in the car, and the pair had agreed that they would certainly go fishing again at the earliest opportunity.

Geoff was no chef, so not wanting to ruin the wonderful fish, he had resolved to ask Janet to cook it when she got home, but he was itching to show it to her and kept going to take a look at it in the fridge. He struggled to stop himself texting her with the news, which would, of course, spoil the surprise.

Now, as he heard her key turning in the front door, he closed the fridge, where he had been looking at the fish one last time, and licking his lips at the thought of the supper to come, went to greet her.

-oo0Ooo-

Caroline was shopping in Waitrose when Bobbie called her, and as she was not far away she suggested they met in the cafe there, so Bobbie could help carry the shopping home in Sybil's little car.

'I wrote it all down, Auntie Caroline,' said Bobbie, opening her new note book.
'The Vehicle Identification Number, or VIN on the car shows the date and country of manufacture, as we know, but the one embedded in the replacement Engine Control Unit, or ECU, has been altered so that the car appears new. Therefore, when anyone plugs a reader into the ECU interface they get the altered information, and it is only if they go scrabbling about reading the VIN number stamped into the car body that the true age is revealed.'

'Algy said that the ECU had been opened and a little printed circuit panel with a tiny connector had been inserted which allowed whoever did it to set the date at whatever they liked.' Bobbie consulted her notes again. 'He demonstrated this by plugging into it and using his equipment to change the date the car appeared to be made to 1982 and then he put it back again where it was. He said you can't do that with the original manufacturer's electronics, but the Chinese fitting to replace them had been doctored so that someone who knew how to do it could disguise its true identity, the engine number, the mileage on the speedometer and so on.'

'Well!' said Caroline.

'Hold on, there is more.' Bobbie turned the page. 'When an imported car is registered by the Driver and Vehicle Licensing place in Swansea, they are given a print-out from the car by the importer which is used to identify the vehicle. These special electronics produce a version of the VIN number for that print-out which is identical to the real one in every detail except for the date of manufacture.'

'And unless the DVLC ask to inspect the vehicle, which they rarely do, that is all they need to issue the paperwork for a UK registration number,' added Caroline. 'Well done, Bobbie. That was a splendid piece of work!'

'Oh, you already knew the last bit, did you?' Bobbie was a little crestfallen. 'Algy told me that he and his brother had imported a couple of cars to use as taxis a few years ago and that is how he knew about the DVLC requiring the print out for registration. They only normally want to see the physical vehicle if it is something unusual like a kit car or a car that has been modified.'

'Your information is very comprehensive, Bobbie, and aligns perfectly with my research. You have just given us the proof we need!'

'Great!' said Bobbie. 'Shall I email you the photographs?'

'Photographs?'

'Yes. I took pictures of the ECU before and after it was removed from Sybil's car, and the insides when Algy opened it up. I put a date stamp on all of them and took a picture of Gary's newspaper on the bonnet of Algy's car to prove the date.'

'Roberta Jane Bassington, I am proud of you. This is brilliant. You are going to make a great investigative journalist! Now let's have a look at those pictures…'

Bobbie handed her phone to her aunt and she started scrolling through the pictures until she found the one of Algy's car.

'What a peculiar looking car,' she exclaimed. 'It is all different colours.'

'That is because it is a "Chekker Cab". Algy's brother Augustus has the white one with the black doors and so on that came off this one and they swap them back when they sell the taxis and buy another pair of black and white ones and do it again. It is their trademark, and it is cheaper than spraying the cars.'

'Good heavens!' said Caroline. 'You have been doing your homework.'

As they finished their coffee Bobbie asked if she was still supposed to take Sybil's car back to her tomorrow.

'Yes, that is fine. If the Police or Trading Standards people want to look at it again they know where to find it. Now let's go home and cook some supper, you must be starving.'

'Until you mentioned it I hadn't really noticed, but yes, I realise now I'm ravenous, and I even forgot to have lunch!'

Chapter 16

As soon as she saw the card on the bouquet of flowers, Bobbie gasped.

'I've been such a fool,' she said.

'That is broadly what David said when he telephoned me earlier, as I was trying to explain,' said Rosy. 'If you recall, we met Carlos at the pub after the cinema. Weasley little fellow with a ghastly smudge of a moustache on his upper lip. He was flocking round Teresa even then, if you could but have seen the signs.'

'And David said that Teresa had dated him?'

'A couple of times, apparently. And it didn't go well. It can't be easy for these three, in a foreign country and all that. I suppose it is only natural for them to stick together as they share a common language and so forth.'

'But then …'

'Then,' said Rosy, looking Bobbie squarely in the eye,

'this loathsome Carlos tried to force his attentions on Teresa and, while she was having none of it and wriggled out of his odious embrace, he doesn't seem to have got the message and won't leave her alone.'

'And that is why she turned to Pedro …'

'To act as her protector, yes, and sort of be in the way all the time so Carlos couldn't get her on her own. David said she is actually quite frightened of Carlos, although if you ask me it would be easy enough to floor a pip-squeak like that with one sharp backhander.'

'And Pedro didn't think that Teresa wanted him to …'

'Pedro was, and is, the most perfect gentleman and stepped up to look after Teresa as a friend until Carlos got the message and left her alone.'

'Oh, my!'

'Indeed, Bobbie, and judging from exhibit A here in front of us, he loves you still, in spite of your behaviour towards him. And because you wouldn't take Pedro's calls or emails he asked Teresa if he could confide in David, and David called me to try to get the message through to you.'

Bobbie picked up the huge bouquet and looked again at the little card.

'I've been rather …'

'Yes, you have, young lady. Now, while you raise Pedro

on the telephone and grovel, I will go and put these in water and see if Caroline needs a hand with supper.'

But Bobbie did not have time to call Pedro before the front door bell rang and, at Rosy's loud shout for her to come immediately as there was someone to see her, she found herself running down the stairs and into the arms of Pedro himself.

-oo0Oo0-

As they said good night to Pedro, curled up now on the sofa under several blankets, it being too late for him to travel back to London, Bobbie drew Caroline into her bedroom.

'Auntie Caroline, I'm afraid I have a confession to make …'

'Don't tell me that after I had such high hopes based on your work today, you have gone and got another job and are leaving me flat?'

'Good heavens, Auntie! There is no way. Being a trainee investigative journalist is much too exciting! No, if you will have me, I'd like to stay. It's just that …'

'What?'

'I'm afraid I have made a rather foolish mistake and I would quite understand if, when you see what I've done, you might decide you don't want to …'

'What have you done, Bobbie?'

Bobbie reached into the drawer on her bedside table and drew out the little "emergency call button" that she had found in the pocket of her jeans.

'I'm really sorry. I forgot to leave it in the house in Kensington when we left and I found it in my jeans pocket today …'

Caroline looked at the little gadget in her hand and then, much to Bobbie's surprise, threw back her head and let out a deep and rolling laugh.

'Auntie?'

'Don't you worry about that, my girl! As it happens I've got to go and see the chap who gave me the keys of the house on Saturday, before I head back to Wiltshire, so I can give it back to him then.'

'Why is it so funny?'

'You remember I told you I stayed in that house once? Well, when I left, I still had the keys in my pocket, so we are both as bad as each other. Of course that was before it was fitted out with all those electronic gadgets.'

'Yes, well, I'm still very sorry. It was a silly mistake … by the way Auntie, you never did tell me why you were staying in that house. Why did you need to use a 'safe house' owned by the Government?'

'Erm … that's a long story, Bobbie …'

'We have all night.'

'Aren't you tired?'

'Desperately, but the joyful reunion with my adorable Pedro has left me buzzing, and although I am physically exhausted, my mind is in a whirl.'

'All right. Hop into bed, young Bobbie, and I will tell you a bedtime story. But be warned it may make your blood run cold and your flesh creep…'

'Those are the best sort,' said Bobbie, pulling the quilt up round her ears.

-ooo0oo-

Janet opened the kitchen window a little wider to finally get rid of the smell of cooking fish.

'Lovely,' said Geoff.

'Quite,' said Janet. 'Next time see if you can catch two. One big one was very nice but a bit of a chore to divide it into two portions.'

'I shall do my very best,' said Geoff, 'although the club impose a limit as to how many fish you can actually remove and you have to put the rest back.'

'Put them back?' exclaimed Janet. 'After going through all that palaver to hook them out of the water, you have to put them back?'

'You do,' said Geoff. 'Perhaps you would like to come

with me next time and have a go yourself.'

'No, thank you very much. It is quite enough for me to cook the fish without having to fiddle about with those rods and flies and things trying to catch them. I should just want to scoop them in with a net.'

'You have no conception of the joy of pitting your wits against nature …'

'Man the hunter …' smiled Janet, 'Well, my brave caveman, are you going to do the washing up?'

-ooOoo-

'On the seventh of February 1987, I was in Dublin,' said Caroline.

'Uh huh,' said Bobbie, wriggling down a little further under the duvet.

'We had gone to a cinema where we planned to meet someone who said he could fix a meeting for us with Adrian Hopkins, who was the skipper of a ship that we were pretty certain was running guns from Libya to the IRA in Ireland. We were right about him, but it took another year for the authorities to catch him, and this was pretty much at the beginning of our investigations into his activities.'

'Guns?'

'Yes. I worked for a big newspaper group in those days in a team who were involved in all sorts of things.

Anyway, as I was saying, we turned up at this old cinema which was all closed up and there was nobody around, so we wandered round to the back to see if our contact was there. It was just as well we did because, as we went behind the back wall, there was one hell of an explosion that blew out the whole front of the cinema.'

'Oh, my goodness!'

'It emerged later that the UFF, that is the Ulster Freedom Fighters had planted an incendiary device there and were presumably aware of our meeting. We were lucky to get away unscathed.'

'So they were trying to blow you up!'

'It would appear so, and when they realised they had missed their target, they issued death threats against all the members of our team.'

'Including you?'

'Yes. So the newspaper rushed us back to England and the Government put us into the safe house in Kensington for three or four weeks until it all died down. There isn't much else to say about it really, but now you know why I stayed in that safe house, and foolishly left with the keys in my pocket.'

'Blimey, you did do some dangerous stuff, Auntie Caroline!'

'Well, I was younger then, and to be honest, that

was pretty scary and was the main reason I left the newspapers and went to work for the BBC in Scotland. So there you are.'

'You don't do that sort of dangerous stuff now, do you?'

'No. Not so much. Don't worry Bobbie, I'm not going to send you anywhere where you might get blown up!'

'I'd go if you wanted me to, Auntie Caroline, you know that…'

'Bless you, child. But don't worry. When I told your mother about offering you a job, I promised I would keep you out of harm's way, and I will.'

As Bobbie was yawning hugely, Caroline tucked her in and wished her goodnight.

-ooOoo-

Chapter 17

As Bobbie had to drive to Woking to take Sybil's car back, she suggested that she could take Pedro to Woking railway station to make his journey shorter.

'Is furry good idea, Bobbie,' he said. 'Save the Pedro some a money too.'

'You didn't think to buy a return ticket, then?'

'I just a desperate see my Bobbie, hang the expense.'

'Oh, Pedro, I'm so glad we sorted all that out,' said Bobbie, unlocking the little car. 'I really am so sorry I didn't trust you.'

'So you say about the million times. But if you want do more of the kiss and make-up, is fine with Pedro!'

'Get in, and we will see about that later,' smiled Bobbie.

'You know it worry me that a maybe you run off when I no looking. No thinking the Pedro leaving the Bobbie, that not gonna happen. I a stick you like the glue.

You not liking the other boys, please, only liking the Pedro.'

'I absolutely promise I only liking the Pedro,' said Bobbie, reaching over to give him a kiss before she started the engine.

-ooOoo-

'So just to be clear, Sybil,' Caroline said, 'they showed you a copy of form V267 … I mean the form that said "Certificate of Newness" on the top, but didn't leave it with you, but they left you a copy of the V355/4 which is the "First Tax and Registration Form", along with a tax form with HMRC on the top?'

'Yes, those are the forms I have here.' Sybil moved the phone to her other hand and checked the papers again.

'Right, well, Bobbie is on her way to you, as I said, and when she gets there can you ask her to take a photo of those forms, clearly showing the numbers, please.'

'No problem. Are you getting somewhere with this now then, Caroline?'

'Yes, I really think I am. Can I say again I'm sorry for having to borrow your car and the inconvenience, but if I'm right I think you might get a visit from the Police soon to take a statement, and the Trading Standards people might like a look at the car.'

'Well, I'm not bothered about that if it stops this happening to anyone else.'

'Look, I don't know if this will happen, but if any other reporters approach you, you will remember what we agreed, won't you, and just direct them to me?'

'Of course, and I do remember what you said about the TV people as well. Do you really think it will come to that?'

'I doubt it, but nothing would surprise me, Sybil.'

'Oh, your niece is here, I just saw the car go past the window.'

'Great. Speak to you later Sybil,'

''Bye, Caroline, and thanks.'

-oooOoo-

'You have to feel slightly sorry for old Cyril Duncan-Browne,' said Geoff. 'He says that mother-in-law of his is already dictating terms before her granny flat is even finished.'

'She is still in the care home, isn't she?'

'Yes, but his wife dragged him along to visit her and she is wanting to pick out new furniture and all sorts.'

'His wife wants new furniture?' Janet was only half listening as she read the instructions for her new washing machine again.

'No, his mother-in-law wants to pick out new furniture for her granny flat, and apparently she will only accept really flowery covers and curtains and so on that come from some posh shop in London. Cyril says it will look ghastly and cost a fortune.'

'I can just imagine her being argumentative and difficult about that,' said Janet. 'Horrible woman.'

'Yes. By the way did I tell you we might have a chance to go and fish for salmon up in Scotland? It will mean a couple of nights away, of course, but Cyril says his wife will come, and you could come too and do some sightseeing or shopping or whatnot with her, while we fish. What do you think?'

-ooOoo-

Chapter 18

'We have got to wrap this up this week,' Caroline was saying.

'I think I have got the file sorted out as you asked,' said Bobbie.

'Good. Now I'm going to call DS Morris and arrange a meeting which I want you to come along to.'

'OK, where will that be?'

'Scotland Yard.'

'What! Really? Actually Scotland Yard in London?'

'That is where he is based, so that is where we will go.'

'Blimey!' said Bobbie.

'Here is the plan ...' Caroline turned her notebook to face Bobbie as they sat at the dining table. "It is likely that things will happen quite fast now, so I want you to make absolutely sure that you keep your car full up with petrol, please.'

'Yes, Auntie Caroline,' said Bobbie, blushing and studying the pattern on the table cloth.

-ooOOoo-

'Wull, I dunno,' said Mr Prentice, sliding his cap back and scratching his head, 'I been working for Janet for years, y'see, and her old mother before her.'

'Yes, but couldn't you fit in both of us? I mean it can't take long to do their garden …'

'That takes quite long enough to keep it looking nice, and I'm s'posed to be retired now. I'm not sure I want to take on any more.'

'You won't reconsider? That is your final word?'

'Yus. I'm afraid so, Colonel Duncan-Browne. I can't see as how I can do it. Mind you, my grandson, young Derek, he might be interested. He is at the …um … Orticulturural College at the moment, and he will soon be out looking for work, like.'

'Well, that's excellent news, Billy! Send him to see me at the earliest opportunity and we will see what can be done.'

'Yus but, oil still need him to help me mow at Janet's, Colonel. I can't have him spending all his time up yours.'

'No, no, I see that. I'm sure we can find a workable

solution, Billy. By the way, would you like a doughnut? I got some from the bakery just now.'

'I'd rather have another look at that special fishing tackle of yours, if it's all the same, Colonel. Got to watch me sugar intake. You really think you could get us a go on that river with the salmon?'

-oo0Ooo-

The wedding plans were coming together nicely.

It was only going to be a simple service, but as Janet had never married, she felt justified in having a proper wedding dress, and she had chosen something really gorgeous.

At least she had thought it was gorgeous, but now the time had come to make a commitment and place the order for the expensive garment she was having doubts, so she asked Rosy and Bobbie to accompany her to the dressmaker's at the weekend to get their opinions. If that went well, she decided she would be bold enough to confirm her decision and pay a deposit.

The little church was booked and the funny old fossil of a priest was engaged to do the essential bits. She and Geoff had had their first wedding practice and the Banns were due to be read.

All very traditional and not at all how Geoff envisaged the proceedings, particularly because, as a Catholic service, there were differences to what he had experienced as a choirboy in the Church of England establishment round the corner from where he grew up, and he had very little recollection of his own first wedding service, which was in a registry office.

But Geoff would go along with anything, at least as far as the wedding was concerned. He kept on saying that he could not believe his luck that Janet should consent to marry him at all, and whatever she wanted was fine by him.

He couldn't help with the choice of dress, of course. But he was enjoying being involved in arrangements for the modest reception, in the posh hotel where they would spend their first night as husband and wife, and she smiled to herself when she thought of him sitting, with his notebook on his knee, checking and re-checking all the details.

-oo0Ooo-

Rosy was busy planning an event too.

Fortunately there was plenty of room at Matravers Hall, and the spacious reception hall was perfect.

Being the main part of the big old house, before it was divided up into seven 'wings' and two apartments, Bobbie's mother enjoyed the run of the original reception rooms, dining room and broad, dramatic, curved staircase which was mentioned in the 'Official

Listing' of the building and could not even be decorated without the permission of the pernickety 'Conservation Officer' at the Local Council.

'If,' she had said, 'they knew about Bobbie's habit of sliding down the polished mahogany banister rail every morning, with a whoop and a holla, they would probably have a fit.'

Bobbie's mother had also said that she had supposed it would be all right to festoon it with bunting or tinsel, because it was temporary, but she had warned Rosy to keep any over exuberant behaviour in check in there, once the party got underway.

The rather grand dining room, with the massive old oak table pushed against one wall for the buffet, would be used for dancing, and the mobile disco chap and the caterers had been booked.

Rosy was also impressed that Mrs Bassington had taken personal responsibility for inviting the owners of the other 'wings' and apartments, out of politeness. She had not been able to contact a couple of them who lived abroad for part of the year, but the others had been understanding, and in refusing their invitations graciously, had expressed the hope that the party would go well, while shaking their heads at what these young people got up to nowadays.
She had even arranged to 'borrow' a few of the parking spaces in the designated areas off the wide drive for the guests when they arrived.

When Bobbie drove her Aunt back to Matravers Hall she would have no inkling that what awaited her there was a surprise birthday party, and with Caroline sworn to secrecy, and accommodation booked for Pedro and some of their university friends at the local pub, everything was coming together splendidly.

-ooOoo-

Chapter 19

'So visiting the prison didn't get us a lot, apart from confirmation that Linda Williams is using the workshop on the Europa Business Estate again and the suspicion that her former cell mate's brother-in-law is mixed up in this in some way.'

'Well, it does mean we now have to move quickly, Jack. If word gets out that we are on to her, Linda Williams will be gone with the wind.'

DS Jack Morris, having been introduced to Bobbie, had asked DC Shaun Phelps to join them, who tapped politely on the door of the little meeting room now.

'Come on in, Shaun,' DS Morris called. 'You know Caroline, of course, and this is her niece, Roberta, or should we call you Bobbie, another Bassington, who has just started working for Caroline.'

After the usual pleasantries, Caroline got down to business.

She spread out photographs on the table of the various Government forms relating to Sybil McDonald's car and some of Bobbie's photographs taken in the workshop, which she had had enlarged and printed at the local supermarket.

'Let me explain how this was done, as I see it,' she said.

Bobbie wrote extensively in her new notebook as Caroline spoke and the policemen asked questions. She wanted to remember how this was presented and to see what questions the policemen were likely to ask.

'Right,' said DS Morris as she finished, 'I've already got the Inspector up to speed with most of this and he has agreed that we can mount a raid at the workshops and arrest whoever is there. We will have the forensic boys standing by, too, and we are trying to book a police photographer, if we can find one who is not off with this flu that is going round.'

'Obviously we want to catch Linda Williams there too, if we can,' said DC Phelps, 'and I've established a sort of pattern as to when she goes there from our surveillance. She is most likely to be there at about half-past ten on a Friday morning, when she seems to be in the habit of getting bacon sandwiches from the cafe for the workers and then she stays in the workshop until about noon, when she leaves.'

'So that gives us our window of opportunity,' said Caroline. 'And nice though it is of her to buy the workers bacon sandwiches, I think that is when we can disrupt the operation most effectively.'

'You are correct, of course, Caroline.' DS Morris looked at her with admiration. 'As you observed, there is a security-locked door on the workshop with an intercom to gain access, but Shaun saw that Linda props it open when she goes to the cafe to make it easier to get back in with an armful of sandwiches and take-away teas. We need someone to take advantage of that and walk in before they can shut the door, otherwise we might have to force an entry, which is just more paperwork. Shaun, can you handle that?'

'No problem, but keep the uniforms out of the way until I am in.'

Bobbie was fascinated by all this and was looking at her aunt now with a pleading look in her eyes.

'I thought Bobbie here could stay in the background with me, taking pictures until you have secured the premises.'

'You know the rules, Caroline, that is fine so long as you stay well out of sight until the arrests are made and I signal for you to come forward. Linda Williams doesn't have a history of violence, but we don't know who else is in that workshop until we have secured it. But yes, don't worry, you will get your scoop. The uniforms will keep any other press away until you have had a good look around.'

'So Friday morning it is then,' said DC Phelps. 'Shall

I ask the Inspector to join us so we can go over the operational points?'

'Erm, no. You show Caroline and Bobbie out while I go and carefully see if I can wheedle him out of his meeting. He is in with the Chief Super and might not be too pleased to be disturbed.'

'Can't we …'

'No, Caroline. You know we have already stretched a point to let you be involved as much as you have been. I will give you a call with the details of where you have to be, and when, as soon as the operational plan is finalised.'

'OK. Thank you, Jack. See you on Friday.'

-ooOoo-

When Sybil McDonald opened the door to the two policewomen and invited them in, she saw the curtains in the bay window of the bungalow opposite twitch.

'This will give her something to think about,' she muttered to herself. 'Nosy old bag.'

'I beg your pardon?' said the younger of the two police officers.

'Oh, nothing. Just thinking aloud about my nosy neighbour watching you arrive,' said Sybil.

'I'm afraid the car does make us rather conspicuous, doesn't it.'

'And the uniforms always get a bit of attention,' smiled the older police woman. 'Now then, perhaps we could start with how you came to buy the car, Mrs McDonald …'

-ooo0oo-

Chapter 20

There was a loud clang as, assisted by her foot, the door shut behind her, and Linda Williams tipped the paper-wrapped sandwiches onto the counter.

'Breakfast, lovelies. Come and get it while its hot!' she called. 'Oh, 'ello?' she said, noticing the man in the suit at the counter for the first time. 'Is somebody helping you, luvvy?'

Stepping behind her swiftly and opening the door to the uniformed policemen now approaching, DC Shaun Phelps said, 'No, but these gentlemen would like a word with you, Linda.'

From where Caroline and Bobbie sat in the little sports car the view was not great.

They could just see part of the gates of the compound and a couple of police cars, but the workshop was obscured by the blank side wall of the cafe and the empty warehouse unit next door, and closer to where they had been told to park. They would not have been aware that anything was happening if Caroline's phone had not registered the receipt of a text message.

A glance at the screen showed DS Morris had sent her just one word, "Now." But it was enough and the pair were out of the car in a trice and sprinting towards the workshop.

Caroline unshipped her huge camera from her shoulder as they approached, and started snapping before she had even had time to see what she was snapping at. Bobbie, taking that as her cue, pressed the video button on her mobile phone and started filming the scene unfolding before them.

As they approached, several men were being led from the building in handcuffs, and at their head, leading the little procession, Linda Williams was being helped into the back of a police car.

As she started to lower herself into the car, for a fleeting second her eyes locked with Bobbie's.
'You!' she said, and resisting the policeman trying to help her into the car for a moment she gathered herself and spat forcibly in Bobbie's direction.

She was too far away to hit her target but she followed it with a stream of vitriol which might have shocked a nice convent-educated girl like Bobbie, and Caroline stepped in front of her protectively.

-oo0Ooo-

There were several work benches with wiring,

components and boxes in front of computer screens in the workshop, and the distinctive slightly acrid smell of hot soldering irons filled the air.

There was a large tower of electronics in a glass fronted cabinet in the middle of the room with wires snaking across the floor. The wires led to a couple of office desks again adorned with computers and stacks of papers, some spilling onto the floor.

There were signs of a struggle as more paper, this time blank but headed with Government logos, had fallen onto the floor near a large complicated-looking printing machine which was humming loudly and was being examined by a pair of dark-suited officials, who DC Morris explained were from HM Customs and Excise.

Over to one side there was a commercial waste bin on wheels, which was being examined by uniformed officers and in which Bobbie recognised several black boxes similar to the one removed from Sybil McDonald's car by Algy Dobbins, in Gary's garage.

But as Caroline headed outside, through two double doors, Bobbie had to rush to catch up.

There, neatly parked against the back fence were five white Nissans, identical to Sybil's, alongside one pale blue, and three grey ones. None had number plates.

In an adjacent building with tall roller doors, Bobbie could see three car lifts, like the one in Gary's garage. Two were idle and empty, but the third was occupied by another pale blue Nissan, this time wearing

British number plates denoting the latest age-related registration numbers.

A little further into this building was an area set aside for car washing and valeting, with all the paraphernalia of that occupation strewn all over the floor.

Through an open back door Bobbie and Caroline could see a large fabric- sided lorry with ramps up to the rear, and with the 'curtains' partially open on one side, revealing yet another pale blue Nissan, complete with the latest number plates, presumably awaiting another car to be loaded behind it for delivery.

Behind that, in the open part of the compound that they could just see when they were in the little sports car, there were three large containers, and they walked towards them now as Bobbie's mobile phone beeped to complain that it would shortly need charging.

Two of the containers had obviously been there a while and the open doors revealed an empty interior.

The third container was the one Caroline had seen being unloaded, and as they approached it now, the two uniformed officers who had been working to open it, achieved success and the doors swung open to reveal a row of small grey Nissan cars, protected from damage by large polystyrene beams or straw filled sacking and with ratchet straps securing them to the floor.

Each had number plates, but were not like those seen in England.

'I knew it!' said Caroline. 'They are Maltese ... See, they all end in a 'K' or a 'QZ' ... That designates them as rental cars in Malta! And I know just who sent them here!'

In between speaking rapidly into her mobile phone and walking quickly back towards the workshop, Caroline told Bobbie over her shoulder to take lots of pictures of these cars, and particularly the number plates.

As she did as she was told, Bobbie hoped and prayed that her mobile phone battery was up to the task. It was going to be tight.

Chapter 21

The mood, in the little sports car, was already pretty jolly as Caroline and Bobbie set off for Matravers Hall.

'I've just realised it is my birthday on Monday. In all the excitement I had completely forgotten all about it. I wonder if somebody will tell Pedro. We should go out for a meal or something.'

'Good heavens!' chuckled Caroline, 'Another birthday! How old will you be this time?'

'Twenty-four … Blimey! That sounds old when you say it out loud!'

'Well, wait till you get to my grand old age then!'

They called at some nondescript offices in Aldershot, near the Army Barracks on the way, and Caroline made Bobbie wait in the car while she took the little "emergency button fob" Bobbie had found in her jeans pocket, now in an envelope, into the reception area.

'Who works in there?' she asked as Caroline climbed

into the car again.

'Oh, just some Civil Servants. Turn right up here then first left at the lights. It is quite a busy junction so take extra care. Remember you have a precious cargo.'

'Precious cargo?'

'Yes, Bobbie. Me!'

-ooOoo-

The story of the car swindle had sold for a good price and then been syndicated across the print networks, and Bobbie watched Caroline conduct the negotiations over the phone and by email with interest.

The Daily Mirror had pushed the bidding up because they wanted an exclusive. When Bobbie asked why, Caroline explained that the photograph she took of one of the little boxes and Gary's newspaper on the bonnet of Algy's car appealed to them as it gave the impression that, with the Daily Mirror in the photo, they had broken the story themselves.

'That sort of self-promoting vanity is typical of some of the red-top newspapers, but in spite of that, we did better selling it via SWNS, the news agency I often use, who gave it a broad spread of exposure. That was how that consumer TV programme heard about it. They are going to interview DS Jack Morris, or his boss, and run a feature on it to make people aware of that sort of scam, apparently.'

'So they are not interviewing you then, Auntie Caroline? After all you did all the work.'

'Ah, yes, Roberta, but as you will learn, it is better for us to stay in the background. If we accept the limelight it is difficult for us to remain unrecognisable, and often invisibility is our best friend. I wouldn't like some of the people I have come across over the years to be able to recognise me!'

'No, I see what you mean. It could get a lot worse than that foul Linda Williams spitting at me, I suppose.'

'You are not to let that bother you, Bobbie. She is going to be out of circulation for a very long time and in many respects is small fry compared to some we may come across. But take my advice and hide behind a camera or something and you remain anonymous.'

'So did you make a lot of money out of the story, Auntie?'

'Pretty good, I must say, and I hope there will be a few spin-offs to produce further income from it. You need have no fear, your salary is adequately covered for now.'

'Oh, I wasn't meaning …'

'I know. Relax. You did really well and I feel it in my bones that you have a bright future ahead of you doing this work, young Bobbie.'

'Not so young on Monday,' Bobbie wrinkled her nose. 'Silly of me to forget about it, but perhaps as you get older, birthdays do mean less.'

'That is how we oldies manage the march of time! Look, slow down a bit, can you. That motorbike you keep over-taking thinks we are in a race.'

'You should have seen Janet's wedding dress. It was beautiful,' said Bobby, changing the subject.

'I think it was lovely of her to ask you to be a bridesmaid. Did you say she also has a maid-of-honour?'

'Yes, that is her old friend Lucy. She is great fun, and Uncle Geoff is like the cat who got the cream!'

'Well, he did rather. I think Janet is delightful.'

'Oh, so do I. We get on famously.'

'Well, there is no need to get on quite as fast as we are going, now Bobbie. You will end up losing your licence and that will really hinder your career.'

'Sorry,' said Bobbie and slowed down.

'Now, there was something I wanted to mention to you,' said Caroline. 'Next week I'm staying with your mother at Matravers Hall, as you know, but the week after that how would you like to have a few days with me up in Scotland at my cottage? We could do a bit of sight-seeing and so on.'

'Yes, please, Auntie, that would be lovely.'

'I do warn you that the shower is rubbish so you won't want to be spending quite so long in there, although there is plenty of hot water. It is heated by solar panels actually … and before you say anything derogatory, yes, we do get enough sun up there north of Glasgow!'

'I've never been to Glasgow,' said Bobbie thoughtfully.

'It's Killearn, actually. In Stirlingshire. The best way to get there is by train to Glasgow Central and then change to go to Milngavie. Let me know your travel arrangements and I'll pick you up at the station.'

-oo0Ooo-

Now, as they turned onto the narrow road leading to the gates of Matravers Hall, just as it was beginning to get dark, Bobbie let out a sigh.

'I always liked coming home to Matravers Hall when I was younger, and there is no doubt that it is a lovely old place, but it is so quiet. I wish it was nearer my young friends. You won't mind if I go back in the morning, will you, Auntie. I really would like to see Pedro.'

'Fine by me,' said Caroline smiling to herself, 'if you can tear yourself away.'

'Good heavens! What a lot of cars!' said Bobbie as they pulled into the gates, 'I don't think I have ever seen so

… Wait a minute! What's that!'

Bobbie pulled the little sports car up as she caught sight of the huge paper banner flapping in the breeze and draped across the wide front porch. It read "Happy Birthday Bobbie" in large red letters, and as she looked, Rosy and Pedro led an explosion of smiling people in party clothes as they burst out of the front door.

-oooOoo-

Epilogue

When they met again, DS Morris explained that in Malta and in Japan, in the ensuing weeks, arrests had been made.

Linda Williams' company was not the only one importing ex-holiday rental cars from Malta, but only her organisation made claims that the cars were new, even if they did cover those claims in the small print they gave the purchasers.

The operation to 'fool' the brain of the car and the Driver and Vehicle Licensing Centre into registering the cars as new, was also unique to Linda's operation.
It emerged that amongst those arrested at her workshop, was a strange, withdrawn young woman who had recently graduated with a first class honours degree in computer science as a software designer.
Because of her autism, mannerisms, and the somewhat awkward way she had of communicating, she had found it difficult to secure mainstream employment. She had been sent to an open prison for

repeated shoplifting offences, as a 'short sharp shock', by an inflexible legal system which had no other ideas as to what to do with her.

That same open prison was where Linda Williams had been sent to serve out the end of her sentence, shortly before she was released, and where she befriended the hapless girl.

It was she who reprogrammed the electronic 'brains' of the cars Linda sold, using a device of her own invention, and when interviewed, she said she did it for the challenge rather than the money, although her bank account swelled considerably as a result of her efforts.

She said what motivated her to keep on doing it was her aim to get quicker and quicker at it, and she kept charts on which she recorded each of the steps involved in a strange hieroglyphic style, timed to the second.

DC Phelps was seconded to a team looking into how Linda financed the operation and they discovered that the initial seed-corn, to buy the first cars, came via Linda's old cell mate, Anne Susan Simmons, whose brother-in-law, owned the workshop and had been involved with Linda Williams in the past.

Linda herself brought the importing expertise, and with a shadowy accountant, who DC Phelps team took some time to track down, she controlled the business overall.

Following DC Phelps tip-off, Caroline got another

story out of that which she also sold quite profitably and with the proceeds, she had a new power-shower installed in her cottage in Scotland, and offered to fund a part-time Post Graduate course leading to a Diploma in Journalism at Roehampton University, for Bobbie.

It had the added attraction of being close to Richmond Park and the college where Pedro was studying, and Bobbie could not believe her luck.

'You will have to work when you are not on the course, though,' she said, I've just got three more leads on really interesting stories and I'll need you to do a lot of the background research for me.'

'I am really looking forward to that,' said Bobbie. 'All of it. Thank you very much, Auntie Caroline!'

'Yes, well, soon enough you can start earning some money and become a proper investigative journalist,' she smiled. 'Then you can keep me in the style to which I shall rapidly become accustomed, young Bobbie.'

-oo0Ooo-

The End ... or is it just the beginning?

Watch out for another Bobbie Bassington Story coming soon!

What's next? Well, there is another new series coming featuring **Bobbie Bassington** who we first met in Double Life Insurance. The first book in the series, **'Bobbie and the Spanish Chap'** and it is out now and joined by **'Bobbie and the Crime Fighting Auntie'**, and the third book in the series, **'Bobbie and the Wine Trouble'** should be released as you read this. These are amusing stories with a twist, that would make great beach reads. They feature the trademark Bob Able lighthearted writing style and engaging 'unputdownable' plots.

If you like Bob Able's distinctive writing style and would like to read more of his work, here is a little more information…..

About the author:

Bob Able is a writer of fiction, thrillers and memoirs and describes himself as a 'part-time expat' splitting his time between coastal East Anglia in England, and the Costa Blanca in Spain.
He writes with a lighthearted touch and does not use graphic descriptions of sex or violence in his books, that is not his style. He prefers to leave that sort of thing to the reader's imagination.

The Bestseller, **'Spain Tomorrow'**, the first book in his popular and amusing memoir series was the **third most popular travel book on Amazon** in late 2020 and with its sequel, **'More Spain Tomorrow'** it continues to attract many good reviews and an appreciative audience in Europe, The United Kingdom, the USA and beyond.

His fictional novels include **'No Point Running'**, **'The Menace Of Blood'** (which is about inheritance, not gore) and the sequel **'No Legacy of Blood'** and are fast-paced engaging thrillers, with a touch of romance and still with that signature gentle Bob Able humour.

His semi-fictional memoir **'Silke The Cat, My Story'**, written with his friend and wine merchant, Graham Austin and Silke the Cat herself, is completely different. Cat lovers adore it and so do readers across the generations. Silke is a real cat. She lives today in the Costa Blanca, in Spain, and her adventures, which she recounts in this amusing book, really happened.

You can find details of how to buy all Bob's books, ebooks and even an **audio book** of '**Silke The Cat, My Story**' and follow him at:
www.amazon.com/author/bobable
Or just enter **Bob Able books** on the Amazon site and the full list should appear. For the Audio book check out **ACX.com**

You can send Bob an email at the address below, perhaps to request details of release dates. The email address is live and will reach him in person.
bobable693@gmail.com

Thank you for reading. You may like to know that Bob regularly contributes a proportion of the royalties from his books to 'The Big C', Norfolk's cancer charity, who have helped Bob with his own cancer battle and who do great practical work to help cancer victims and promote research.

Find out more at:-
www.big-c.co.uk

Thanks to Andy Crabb, Bobbie's first fan, for his inspired help and proofreading.

Cover photo credit: Dominic Sansotta. and Ivan Kazlouskij.

Please leave a review on Amazon or Goodreads if you liked this book.

-ooo0oo-

Disclaimer:
Note: All rights reserved. No part of this book, ebook or manuscript or associated published or unpublished works may be copied, reproduced or transmitted by any means, electronic, mechanical, photocopying or otherwise, without the prior written permission of the author.
Copyright: Bob Able 2022

The author asserts the moral right under the Copyright, Design and Patents Act 1988 to be identified as the author of this work.

This is a work of fiction, Any similarities between any persons, living or dead and the characters in this book is purely co-incidental.
The author accepts no claims in relation to this work.

**Incidentally, Bob is looking for a new publisher
and a 'literary agent' to represent him ...
any ideas?**

Printed in Great Britain
by Amazon